no
bad
deed

copyright

playlist

Blood and Bones	Warpath.	Prisoner
The Blake Robinson	*Tim Halperin/Hidden Citizens.*	*Raphael Lake/Aaron*
Synthetic Orchestra		*Levy/Daniel Murphy*
Numb.	Don't Be Shy	You Never Know
Sabrina Claudio.	*Tiësto/Karol G*	*KNGDAVD*
I Love You	She Used to Be Mine.	Feral Love
Alex & Sierra	*Chloe Adams.*	*Chelsea Wolfe*
Get Free.	You Don't Own Me	My Boyfriend's Back
Whissell	*Grace/G-Eazy*	*The Angels*
Overpass Graffiti	Fool.	Bad Dream
Ed Sheeran	*Nostalghia/Tyler Bates.*	*Ruelle*
Monsters	Dark Side.	Marry You
Ruelle	*Bishop Briggs.*	*Bruno Mars*
Shivers	Outrunning Karma.	Scars
Ed Sheeran	*Alec Benjamin.*	*Boy Epic*
Angry Too.	Perfect	
Lola Blanc.	*Ed Sheeran*	

Author's Note

CONTENT WARNING
Vulgar speech, explicit scenes (including noncon), drug use, violence, gore, and possibly a myriad of other aspects that may not be suitable for all readers may appear in this book.

If this list isn't comprehensive enough, please read reviews or check my reader's group: Emma's Author Stalkers on Facebook.

REVIEWS
Please do consider leaving a review as it helps others determine if this is the right book for them. In addition to that, the more interest there is in a particular series, the more likely that it will get bumped up in the schedule. (If authors don't know

how you feel about a book/series, we don't know what you'd like to see next.)

PIRATING

Please don't be a pirate, it really does have an impact. It is theft, so don't do it!

Miss Angela 'Angel' Christine—I was in the middle of writing this when I heard you were gone, taken from us far too soon. You always asked me for signed copies of my books, not that I was too keen on outing my pen name at the time. But I haven't been able to type the word 'angel' without thinking about you, so here it is. This one is for you. Your memory will live on—in the adventures we shared growing up and in the hearts and minds of your children and loved ones. Love you to the moon and back again, little cuz, until we meet again.

My name is Eden Moretti.

After leaving the Carlotti heirs for my own safety, unsure of if, or when, I'd return, I set out on a journey of self-discovery and healing. But my travels abruptly ended when I discovered the men I couldn't ever fully put out of my mind making national news. I watched from hundreds of miles away as they were arrested.

For murdering the two dirty cops. For my alleged kidnapping.

I knew it was either a ploy to flush me out or a convenient lie to put them away, but I made the call to Vinnie anyway. Now I'm on my way home to try to rescue my original bad habits.

Even though I was on my way to help exonerate them, I was too late to save them from our enemies. They hurt my men, but now I'll have my revenge.

If they want to escape my wrath, well, they'd better kill me first.

No Bad Deed is a dark mafia reverse harem and the epic conclusion to the Bad Habits Duology. HEA, spice, and everything not so nice, are guaranteed.

prologue
blood and bones

The hollow, metallic scrape of an object dragging across the pavement followed me as I stumbled through the warren of alleyways, tripping over trash until I ran into a dead end. I'd left a blood trail a blind man could follow, and I knew I wasn't going to make it over the top with a hole in my leg. Fucking with that whore had brought down a whole heap of shit, and now I was paying the piper.

I turned to face my approaching death, hoping for mercy, but it was a pipe dream. That I'd been fucked over had been made more than clear as soon as Evans had tried to take me out in the strip club. There was nowhere left to run.

"I was only following orders!" I shouted at the man who was coming ever closer.

"What part of 'Eden Moretti is off limits' did you

not understand?" he demanded as he leveled his gun on me. I'd lost my own when I'd been flushed out of my hidey-hole...about the same time I'd picked up the wound in my leg that was leaving a puddle of red so dark that it almost appeared black in the shadows around me.

"That wasn't me. It was Evans!" I shot back, voice high with panic. I wasn't getting out of this no matter what I said. I didn't even know how he'd found me in the first place. Rumors had run rampant for weeks, and the newest one popped up yesterday, claiming that my partner, Evans, had turned up after being tortured with his throat slit.

"You took her out of the house. You chose to be a part of it—and don't worry, Evans got his, just like you're going to get yours. I'll let you decide if your *exit* is going to be as dramatic as his." The man held up the business end of an aluminum bat in his other hand, and while I couldn't be sure it was the same one, the threat was enough to make my asshole pucker. "You tell me who has the hit out on her, give me *all* the players, or I'm going to give you the same treatment I gave your little friend."

Vividly, I remembered the stripper's echoing screams as Evans played his sick games. I decided then and there that I'd rather go out with some dignity and a hell of a lot less pain. Besides, when I was dead, it wouldn't matter if I was a rat.

"It was DeLuca," I rasped out as my vision went

spotty, easily giving up my boss since I was faced with a more imminent threat. If the lightheadedness was any indication, the blood loss was going to do me in soon anyway. "He has almost the entire precinct and a good deal of both crews in his pocket." My assailant didn't seem surprised, and with a nod I took as thanks, he pulled the trigger.

one

warpath

Tony

"Sir," came through the intercom in my office, "we have a problem out here. There are cops wanting to speak with you." The guard's voice came through, heavy with reluctance at having to be the one to bear the news. He was probably shitting bricks at the possibility of being rounded up and taken into custody, but lucky for him, he wasn't high enough on the food chain to bother with, at least not yet.

I held the button down, asking, "About what?" When there was no answer in return, I checked the surveillance to find my men at the gate being held at gunpoint and frisked. At the same time, a text lit up my phone, filling me in on exactly what they wanted. I cursed up a storm as I stalked into the hall, yelling for the others to alert them to our newest situation after having barely taken care of the last one. Vanni met me first, with Marco not far behind. "Get Santos and call up to the house. We need to make sure this place is clean. Fucking cops are at the front gate with a warrant, and from what I just saw on the video feed, they aren't going to wait patiently for admittance."

"On it," my brother reassured me as he pulled out his phone. "They couldn't have waited until morning, though? I'm fucking beat," he griped.

Looking as tired as I felt, Vanni veered off to handle his part of the preparations—clearing the security footage and disabling the system. After the dirty cops were able to waltz in and Eden was taken, from our own fucking house no less, we'd set plans for just this situation. We weren't stupid; they wouldn't leave us holding our dicks in our hands this time. All of us had known someone would eventually make a move against us, trying to take us out of the equation. Personally, I'd expected it a bit sooner.

I agreed with his sentiment wholeheartedly, tired myself, but at least we had the cover of darkness in our favor. It made removing, and then later replacing, the few things to be hidden a simpler task.

Marco kept pace with me, his limp barely noticeable until I thought he'd forgotten I'd told him to get Santos. But as we neared the end of the hall, he slowed.

"Is he in there *again*?" I asked, coming to a stop with a worried stare at the closed door. At Marco's nod, I shook my head. There wasn't time to mess with it. Santos and his new propensity to sleep in Eden's room was a massive red flag, but so far, that was all he was doing. No fighting, no women, no booze. He did what was asked of him and worked out; other than that, he spent most of his time holed up doing who knew what. "Get him out of there, quickly, and ditch the hardware."

Marco winked, giving me a salute before beating a fist on the bedroom door. "Yo, Santa, get your jolly ass up. I'm coming in!" Again, all I could do was shake my head. The man had a screw loose, or four, and if he kept fucking with Santos, he was liable to get a few more knocked out. At this point, our enforcer was nothing more than a lit fuse away from going off.

"We didn't fucking kidnap, Edie, you lying piece of shit!" Marco shouted as he was cuffed and forced none too gently into the back of a squad car. It all happened amid flashes and a line of reporters clamoring to get through the gate and around the police cruiser blocking the entrance. They all wanted to witness our arrest and show just how far the Carlottis could be taken down. We were far enough back that they probably wouldn't pick much up on their mics, but they weren't the only ones we had to worry about. It was a fifty-fifty chance whether the officers were wearing body cams like they were supposed to, and if they were, I was sure the footage would be leaked soon enough.

"Marco, shut it!" I snapped at him as my own hands were directed behind me. The clicking zip of the metal cuffs came a second after the cold, unyielding material hit my wrists. He fucking knew better than to run his mouth, but a small part of me couldn't blame him, even I had to admit that their bullshit charges were far-fetched. Conspiracy this, kidnap that, and...a double homicide that I knew nothing about. At the moment, I couldn't exactly ask the others if they'd done it without telling me. Someone had found and taken out the two dirty cops who had hurt Eden and shot Marco, but as far as I was aware, it wasn't any of us.

"You want to tell me where she is, then? Or how to contact her?" the cop asked Marco, a sly smirk on his face. He knew there was no way in hell we'd let them anywhere near her, not that we even had any idea where she was at.

Vanni could probably find out if he really wanted to, and maybe he was already quietly keeping tabs on her, but he'd never say a damn thing unless she was in trouble and he couldn't get to her himself. Little brother was all in with her, just as Marco blatantly was, but I thought he was trying to hide it until he knew me and Santos were on the same page. I was, and Santos had likely come to his own conclusions by now with the way he was acting, but I had decided to wait until I could tell Eden directly before I let anyone know I was as hung up on her as they were.

"Is that the only way you can get a girl's number?" Marco taunted in return. He was going to get his ass kicked before we even got through processing. I sighed as the cop ignored him, slamming the door on anything else my mouthy cousin might have to say.

I glanced at my father as I turned and dropped down into the back of the squad car. He gave me a nod of reassurance, already on the phone and barking orders. I was sure the attorneys would have us out by morning at the latest. This was a minor inconvenience at best, and I didn't know what they hoped to gain by it.

As the cavalcade that had come to arrest the four of us turned around and headed out, I hoped that Eden had the sense to lay low. No doubt her picture was about to be plastered across national news stations. A small, selfish part of me contradicted that, wanting her home where she belonged, but I squashed that thought down and buried it deep. It wasn't safe for her, or any of us really, until the city was firmly back under the Families' control and Santos' father was dead.

Dad and the head of the Finellis had spent the

last month cleaning house and shoring up their truce —nothing like a third player trying to usurp the seat of power to bring out the ruthless dons in fully united force.

As we were taken into the precinct, Detective Fields came slamming out with an empty holster in hand and fury pinching his features into a scowl. He'd stepped up for Eden, and again today, even though he'd rather have nailed our balls to the wall than join forces with the same people he wanted to put away. I hated to admit it, but the dude was a good cop. Too bad we were on opposite sides of the line.

The cops that led us in smirked as he went past, giving him shit about being suspended. Despite being sure he saw us, he didn't even attempt to make eye contact, and the first inkling that shit was about to go down crept through my mind.

"Looks like you're losing your cop buddies all over the place," the officer jeered, holding my elbow just tightly enough to pinch. I made a mental note to teach him a lesson after all of this was over. We couldn't let this disrespect stand without setting a bad precedent. Also, with only Fields' text to warn us, I had to wonder what had happened to our other contacts, and why we weren't aware of them disappearing.

I didn't bother responding—it wasn't worth it—and thankfully, Santos, Vanni, and Marco were also keeping their mouths shut as we were paraded through the precinct like living trophies. And I supposed we were.

A sense of relief filled me at seeing our attorneys coming in as we were taken individually to have our fingerprints, scars, and tattoos recorded. By the time I made it into an interrogation room to have my statement recorded, I had gathered that I wasn't actually going to be getting out of there for a while.

They seemed to be dragging the whole process out, and I was getting impatient to be done with the farce. They didn't have shit on us. Nothing concrete at any rate. It was either a gimmick to buy time, or maybe to wear on us in the hopes that one of us would lose our temper, but whatever the reason, their ability to do so without repercussions was a concern.

My suspicions were confirmed once the charges were leveled at us, or at least me, though I assumed it was the same with the others. Supposedly, there was a witness who said they had seen all four of us leaving the scene of not one, but *both* former officers' murder scenes. As if that weren't enough, Eden hadn't turned up yet, so she was considered a missing person, with all of us as the prime suspects for her disappearance. I was threatened with more than just kidnapping charges. If they were able to find any shred of evidence that suggested otherwise, I'd be up on another suspected murder charge. I also knew they weren't above manufacturing that evidence after this bullshit.

The thought occurred that they might not have to make anything up at all, and I prayed that she was still okay, that she would use the burner phone to touch base with someone, because if they'd found her and harmed her at all, they were all fucking dead. I'd level the fucking building and anyone in it. With a sense of surreality, I watched as my attorney shook his head and got to his feet as it was declared that I'd be held until I could see a judge to petition for bail. *I can't believe this shit is happening.*

After an uncomfortable, sleepless night on cots, in open cells without any privacy, morning finally came. We weren't in the same one together, but we were near each other, enough that we could at least see that we were all okay. It was better than *not* knowing, but I was still waiting for the punchline to this joke of an arrest.

It was only a matter of time until we had our arraignment and could get out on bail—unfortunately, it was enough time to give the guards and other inmates the chance to execute their plan. Bring the Carlottis down another peg.

We were taken to the showers and given the hotel-sized toiletries, but we never got a chance to use them. The guard who was supposed to be watching the open showers, shut the door after we filed in, drawing his firearm and keeping it steadily pointed in my direction. It didn't take a rocket scientist to figure out that we were about to be in for the fight of our lives, yet what happened after, I could have never predicted. It just wasn't something that was done, not to us anyway, and it wasn't something we had ever been interested in doing to others.

"You'd better kill us all now," I warned the cop as cold fingers of dread gripped my heart. Impotent white-hot fury burned through the rest of me, and for the first time, I felt the helplessness of our situation.

"I don't think you understand, Antonio. The Families' reign is over. A new regime is taking control, and you can't do shit about it." I committed his face to memory because I damn well *would* be doing something about it if we made it out of here alive, but he only smirked under my glare before tipping his head. "Hurry up. I have other shit to do."

Santos was grabbed first, dragged back into an empty toilet stall with an arm around his throat. As he yelled a garbled mess of profanities, his eyes locked on mine, promising pure retribution. He lunged forward, nearly throwing off his assailant, but then his eyes widened with disbelief, swiftly followed by pain. His grunts sounded out in time to the jerking of his body before he was released and allowed to slide down the wall. He immediately hunched over, clutching at his side—and he wasn't getting back up. It all happened so fast that at first, it was hard to register what had occurred, but then an inmate stepped around Santos with a bloodied, sharpened pick in his hand. My focus remained on my enforcer, though, my disbelieving gaze tracking the red rivulets running between his fingers to puddle around him.

Not caring about the guard, I went for my best friend, only to come up short at the snick of a blade and a burning strip on my throat.

"Not so fast, Tony, we're not finished with you yet." The voice wasn't familiar, but the man behind me spoke as if he knew me, and I watched with angry impotence as Vanni and Marco were subdued. Marco took a bit more effort for them to get down, dishing out several blows that would no doubt leave a mark until he took a kick to his injured leg, which buckled, allowing him to be brought roughly to his knees. "Did you know the Finellis took my sister, but your father did nothing about it? The 'peace' was kept, and she was forced to marry the bastard that had picked her up off the street on the way home from work. You see," he prattled on as droplets of blood littered the pale gray front of my baggy shirt, "there are many of us that have a bone to pick with you and your family, and the Finellis are next." With his declaration, his blade settled more firmly against my skin until it was difficult to breathe without chancing slitting my own throat.

Vanni was shoved forward, lip busted but still defiant, until he ended up before me, not close enough to reach, but enough to taunt me. Another inmate kicked behind his knees as the first shoved his shoulders down, making him kneel on the grimy floor that no amount of bleach would ever get white again. Dread pooled in my gut when the guard came forward to press the muzzle of his gun to Vanni's temple. *They're going to kill my brother.*

I almost didn't care what it took to free him, but the thought of offering myself up in his stead was derailed by Marco's own shout of denial. His demand to take my brother's place preempted my own as he must have come to the same conclusion that we were about to witness an assassination. His protest on Vanni's behalf quickly turned into a groan of pain, making me accept that I had no way to stop whatever was about to happen. I had to assume we would all likely be dead soon, anyway.

"Do you think he'll cry like my sister did?" the man that held me whispered harshly in my ear, and then I felt my blood drain from my face at his meaning. He wasn't going to kill us, not yet, but he was going to have his retribution. Not even a moment later, Vanni was shoved onto all fours. Then the ripping of fabric came harsh and loud thanks to the acoustics in the tiled room, drowning out the thundering pulse in my ears. "DeLuca sends his regards." His statement only added to the staged performance we'd unwittingly been brought into. In a hard voice, showing no remorse, I dared to speak out.

"You're all fucking dead, even if you don't know it yet. I'll kill you all, including your entire fucking family." Vanni's eyes met mine, not with fear, but with a hardened resolve that promised the same.

two

prisoner

Vanni

I held Tony's gaze until my face was ground into the cold, damp floor, bringing the reality of my situation crashing down around me. I struggled until my head was yanked up and slammed down once more, splitting my eyebrow, and then I focused on a crack in the tile, not looking up again. Disbelief coursed through me at what they planned to do, but the reality of my ass hanging out while Santos bled out on the floor and I was made into their newest prison bitch was only compounded by my brother and cousin being forced to helplessly watch it all. They'd obviously been hired to teach us a lesson; the entire warrant and arrest were bogus, which we already knew, but that didn't matter anymore. This was no longer an irritation. This was a message that they could get to us no matter what. That they could do what they wanted without fear of retribution...that we were no longer the top of the food chain. And it was made loud and clear as I was violated. I barely managed to hold in the shout, only letting out a gasp to betray my pain when pure fire rammed its way into my asshole.

I could hardly hear Marco shouting above the buzz in my ears as I tried not to be a pussy about being ass-raped, but fuck, it was unpleasant. During the soul-rending agony, a whisper rose above my internal screams... *They did this to her.* If Eden could survive, overcoming who knew how many violations, I could too. But as it went on and on, I wasn't sure how she wasn't broken into a million jagged pieces that would never fit back together properly. When the fucker came in my ass, the burn alone was bad enough, but he had to accentuate the pain and mortification by slapping it like a fucking horse on the flank. I refused to acknowledge the wet slide of fluid slipping from me to track down my thighs until it hit the tatters of my pants and underwear. If I did, I would lose my fucking shit, and I had no intention of breaking when Edie had been able to keep it together.

I thought it couldn't get worse than being sodomized in front of the others, in front of my *brother*, but the rapist piece of shit cackled as he walked away. "Look at that pussy all broke in and stretched out. Who's next?"

My cheeks flamed in embarrassed fury as I

vowed I'd gut the sick fuck as soon as I had an opportunity. But my ass flinched at the thought of enduring more. I'd do it to save my family, but it might just kill me. *How can I face any of them after this?*

The first must have been the smallest, for the next made me certain that I'd never sit right again. He barely managed to grunt his way to completion before the guard declared time was up, and that we had five minutes to shower before he came back to fetch us for court. He knew damn well we wouldn't all be making it on time, and I wasn't sure Santos would make it at all, but we were left alone in the bathroom to straighten ourselves out.

With the agony my ass and insides were in, I wasn't sure I could stand, but I knew I couldn't stay there, kneeling with my junk hanging out and blood and cum leaking out of my alarmingly slack sphincter. Tony came to help me up until Marco could hobble over to take his place, then my brother immediately went for Santos, who didn't look good at all.

"Tony, is he breathing?" I rasped out, throat dry and tight from holding in my screams. But Tony didn't answer until we made it over to where he had Santos laid out on the floor, the shallow stab wounds in his side exposed.

When Tony applied pressure to the sluggishly bleeding punctures, a groan from our scarred-up friend and enforcer sent relief coursing through me.

"I think he'll be alright if we can get him help," Tony announced, voice harsh and rough with emotion. "Marco, think you can manage something?" he asked after a glance at me, one that traced my disheveled state with more than guilt or regret... There was pity, too. Apparently, it was something neither of us could deal with at the moment, and I was grateful when he turned his attention elsewhere.

Marco nodded at Tony without comment, grim determination on his face as he made for the door after easing me onto the floor with a shoulder squeeze of support. I couldn't sit flat, but I pretended that no one would notice, and at least it covered my aching ass.

Eden

The trip back to New York was a slow one. I wasn't sure that my new ID would hold up to airport security, so I had to opt for driving. Vinnie had warned me to stay low, that it wasn't safe to be recognized without security in place, so drive-thrus and pay-at-the-pump services were my new best friends.

I doubted I would be too recognizable now

anyway. The picture the news outlets were circulating weren't exactly flattering, with my face gaunt and the quality grainy, thanks to what appeared to be old footage of Danny's. It did make me wonder what else could be floating around if someone had the insurance videos he'd kept for blackmail. It wasn't something I could worry about, but I would be warning Vinnie about it as soon as we had a chance for a sit-down.

With my nerves ramping up, I pulled into the pitted lot of the precinct where the guys were being held. I'd hoped for a chance to visit while I was there, but the first order of business was to exonerate them on the kidnapping charge. To do that, I had to find the attorneys who were supposed to meet me. No way in hell would I be walking into a police station without them. Not willingly, anyway.

After cruising around the perimeter of the lot, my attention was caught by two men standing on either side of a high-end luxury car. From what I could tell with the distance between us, they were the attorneys I was looking for. One of them stood just over the white line, holding the parking space, presumably for me, when I turned down their aisle.

As I pulled up to roll my window down, their gazes locked on me, both alert and aware enough that I briefly wondered what had them so jumpy. *But let's be real, the entire city is probably sleeping with one eye open based on the news reports I've caught the last few days.* When I slipped off my sunglasses, recognition lit the eyes of the man closest to me. With a nod, he gestured for his companion to step back to let me pull into the parking space.

Before I could get out on my own, the man had already come around to my door to open it for me, and despite recognizing them from the pics Vinnie had sent, it still had alarm bells ringing. The basic instinct from years of experience was hard to squash, but at least it had kept me alive. Doing my best to ignore my unease, I thanked him and stepped out, pulling my purse with me by the strap without turning my back.

He must have noticed my apprehension, for he stepped back and loosely held his hands out in plain sight. With a nod to his companion, the other man immediately went wide around the back of the sedan, letting me keep an eye on them both.

Slightly flustered that I'd been so obvious, but not a bit apologetic, I slipped my sunglasses onto my head and kept the open door between me and them.

"Miss Moretti, I'm Blaine, and this is my colleague Ezra. We're from the same firm that represents Mr. Carlotti." Seeing that I wasn't about to move, a small grin quirked one side of his lips as the other man came to stand next to him. "Just a moment, let me get him on the phone."

Almost immediately, Vinnie's familiar voice

came from the speaker. "Is she there yet?" he demanded before Blaine could speak.

I decided to answer for him. "I'm here, Vinnie. Just had to be sure someone hadn't cloned your phone or kleptoed it."

With a sigh that held a hint of what I thought was amusement, Vinnie relayed his orders. "You're good, Eden, just get it over with and get home. The boys are on their way."

Wait, what? "On their way? What the fuck is going on? Why am I here if they're out?" *Would Vinnie set me up?* I didn't think so, not after everything, but if it came down to me or his family... My gaze flitted from one man to the other while I contemplated how quickly I could get the door shut and locked. Not that that would stop them for long if they were planning anything.

"The matter has been kept quiet until I could get them out on bail. There was an...incident, and the attorneys were able to get them released because of it. Let Blaine and Ezra fill you in. I need to get down to the house and meet them." With that evasive nonsense, he disconnected, leaving me to either go through with my end or hightail it.

"Well?" I demanded as Blaine put his phone away.

He glanced around, checking for anyone within earshot, and then dropped the news that should have been relayed immediately. "Misters Carlotti and

DeLuca sustained various and substantial injuries during an altercation and have been released on house arrest pending their trial." My stomach clenched while a vise seized my spine until a sharp, stabbing pain radiated through my barely healed torso. The driving and stress had taken their toll, and this wasn't helping. "Miss Moretti, are you alright?" The man—Blaine—asked with concern in his voice. He started forward when I didn't immediately answer.

"Fine," I gasped out, forcing the air through my aching chest until I could form something more complex. "Ribs aren't used to all the activity yet. Let's get this over with. I need to get back to the estate." Seeing the guys for myself was a top priority; I didn't like how the subject of their injuries was being danced around.

Ezra finally broke his silence, obviously done with the holdup as well. "I need whatever I.D. you have on you or anything that doesn't say Eden Moretti. As far as the legal system is concerned, the only official documents you have are a social security card, a birth certificate, and an expired driver's license. Anything else you show up with is going to have them jumping to bring you up on charges. We don't need to have you arrested too." His quiet voice held a direct authority I felt inclined to listen to, one that had me doing a double-take and reassessing the pecking order. It didn't matter now, but maybe it was something to file away for later. You never knew what information could come in handy.

"Sure," I agreed, then set about digging my wallet out before deciding better. I just took the car keys out and handed them to him.

"You won't be needing those either," he informed me as he walked around to stow my purse in the car they'd arrived in. "A driver will come and take it back to the estate. You don't technically have a driver's license, remember?"

Fucking hell, I can't even drive back out of here. We were probably being watched already, and the paranoia that we'd been overheard ran rampant through my mind. With my anxiety ramping up and an infrequent craving for something to soothe it, I tossed the keys to Ezra and gestured for Blaine to lead the way. *Time to get this shit done.*

The fucks tried to hold my ass as a person of interest since I had motive and couldn't exactly verify my whereabouts without giving up the name I'd used, but they also didn't have anything tying me to the murders. With some vaguely threatening language from Blaine about the kidnapping bulletin being entrapment and mentions of the internal investigation they'd only just gotten through regarding the deceased officers, they let me go with a warning to stay in the state.

The last part was perfectly fine by me, but I wanted to know how the hell they hadn't gotten more than a cursory investigation when Internal Affairs was supposed to be an impartial third party. And how the fuck any of us could hope to survive the escalating war if our enemies had such an advantage. But first things first, I needed to get to the estate to see the guys and check in with Vinnie.

And after that, well, I had my own ideas on how to find the real culprit for the murders *and* make them confess.

three

numb

Eden

As we pulled through the gated entrance of the Carlotti estate, I tensed with anticipation and rubbed my sweaty palms across my legging-clad thighs. This wasn't how I'd imagined coming back, and I'd dreamed up *many* scenarios revolving around just that. And half as many about not coming back at all, but as the car came to a halt in front of the guys' house, I realized there was no way I'd have been able to stay away permanently. Being there felt too right.

I was out of the car, my purse over my shoulder, before either attorney had their seatbelt off. Impatience and worry eclipsed nearly anything else, but I managed to quickly thank them, telling them to call if needed, then shutting the door and power walking to the house.

Barely two steps inside, I almost ran over Doc; he

27

was already on his way out with his equipment case in hand. He started to reach into his jacket for a gun, only relaxing when recognition hit.

"Miss Eden, I was just wondering when you'd be arriving." His greeting held warmth, but his expression was all worry as he looked me up and down before muttering, "At least *you* don't seem to be in need of my services this time."

At the reminder, I took stock of the area I could see, but we were alone. I figured one of the guys would have been around, and that just made my impatience to find them rear up again.

"Hey, Doc. And no, I'm good," I offered with a small smile. "The guys upstairs?" I asked with a head tilt in the general direction of the stairs. When he paused and frowned, my concern spiked. "They *are* here, right?"

"Yes, but maybe I should call Tony first. Eden, there's been an incident, and..." He shrugged as if unable, or unwilling, to explain further.

Mind made up to hunt them all down, I reassured the doctor and moved into the house, intent on making a headcount. "No worries, Doc. I'll figure it out. See ya around, yeah?"

Without waiting for a reply, I went straight for the hall with the stairs, a sense of coming home filling me as I neared my bedroom...that had the muffled tones of a woman's voice coming out of it. My intense need to find the guys veered with my discovery, turning to insta-rage. I couldn't believe they'd given my room away, let alone to another woman. *I'll fucking kill her while they watch.* Mind made up on my course of action, I straightened my shoulders and stalked in with my head held high. She'd never think I was about to drown her in the toilet the second I was close enough to grab her skanky ass. And she'd better have her fucking clothes on.

"Mr. DeLuca, please wait for my assistance!" The exasperated voice belonged to the woman who was trying to get Santos unhooked from a monitor, something he was decidedly not planning to do since he was already attempting to climb out of the bed.

Good one, Eden. You were gonna kill a nurse. My skin heated as I realized I'd massively jumped to the wrong conclusion. And that Santos was in *my* bed.

"I leave for five minutes, and you manage to steal my room, huh?" Two sets of eyes landed on me, but there was only one person in the room I cared about, given I'd decided not to murder the help.

"Why are you here? You were supposed to stay away," he greeted me, accusation sitting heavy in gaze. But then his glare relaxed, along with the ruined bits of skin, and something like relief coated his next words. "And I'd say it was a lot longer than five minutes, angel."

The instinct to rebuff the endearment that fell so easily from his lips reared up, but I squashed that fucker down, refusing to fall into old patterns. *Begin as you plan to proceed.* It was the plan, and I wasn't deviating from it. I wanted the boy who'd loved me, that I loved in return, back. It was too late for the kids we'd been, but it wasn't too late now. Not if I had anything to say about it. So I shrugged and moved into the room, closing the door behind me and setting my purse on the dresser while I contemplated if I should offer to help or not.

"You all weren't supposed to go down for me taking off either, so I'd say neither of us held up our end." My attention was on the nurse, who was studiously ignoring our interaction. It was sort of amusing to watch her play statue while holding the lead for the machine he was attached to. "Besides," I added, cutting my eyes to Santos, "I was invited back."

His own briefly closed as he muttered, "Of course you were." And a bit louder, he added, "I'll be discussing this with Vinnie, but I doubt you'll leave willingly now?"

The grin couldn't be denied even with him sitting there like a pissed-off invalid. He knew I wasn't about to tuck tail and hide again. "My vacation was fun, but it's over now, so let's just skip the argument. You seem to be trying to get up, and I'm worried your helper is going to get a cramp if she doesn't move soon."

As if that was all it took to put her back into motion, she resumed her attempt to get him to wait.

"I'll have you unhooked in just a moment, and then I can grab the chair—"

"I'm not using the fucking chair. Unhook me, or I'm doing it myself," he demanded, daring the nurse to contradict him.

She didn't say another word. Instead, she pursed her lips and finished by draping the cords around his neck and rolling his IV pole closer to him. But when she went to assist him in standing, he shooed her away with a glare.

Actually feeling sorry for the chick, I stepped up to intervene. "Come on, you stubborn ass, obviously you have something serious going on if Doc left you like this. Why aren't you in a hospital, anyway?"

I thought the nurse was going to object for a moment, but she quickly decided to let me bear the brunt of Santos' ire.

"I can use the bathroom just fine if you'd both quit hovering," he snapped, even as he let out a grunt when he tried to bear his own weight. "Why don't you go find Tony? Let him know that you're here and need a room. Let me piss in peace."

As he leaned forward, the back of his t-shirt rode up, revealing the stark white edges of his dressing sitting above the low-slung sweats he had on. "What the fuck happened, Santos?" It was my turn for demands, and I decided he could just deal with it while I figured out if I needed to get one of the guys to come help him. He didn't try to stop me as I pulled the bottom of his shirt up to find a rectangle covering part of his back and most of his side. My imagination went wild with images of what the wounds looked like underneath the pristine gauze.

I felt more than saw Santos glance up at me, and whatever my expression held had him immediately reassuring me. "It's not as bad as you're thinking. I got lucky; the idiot had shitty aim."

I moved my stare from his injury to the cobalt eyes filled with guilt and anger. It reminded me a lot of how he had looked after he found out what his father and my mother had done. My fear mounted, worrying that injuries might not be the only issue here. Wetting my dry lips, I asked the question I should have brought up sooner.

"Are the others okay?" If anything, his guilt inten-sified, and my hands tingled with the surge of anxiety wrecking my nervous system as I awaited his response.

"They're more mobile than I am at the moment, but I'm not sure any of us are 'okay.'" That seemed to be all I was going to get since the nurse fumbled something on the supply cart, reminding us both that we had an audience. "But really, I need to piss, and you need to go. Doc set me up as a precaution, said I could come off all this tomorrow as long as I continue to improve." The abrupt change of topic was blatant, but I couldn't fault him for it. Weak wasn't some-thing Santos could stand to be. While I'd let him be and not force my help upon him, I wouldn't chance him making his injuries worse.

"I'll go, if you let your nurse at least help you walk." My ultimatum was met with a sharp glare, but backing down wasn't on my agenda.

"Fine," he gritted out, annoyance radiating from his tensed jaw down to his sexy, bare feet. Seriously, I wasn't sure if I'd ever noticed as a teen, and feet weren't my fetish, but Santos had remarkably nice ones for a dude. "Eden, I said fine. Stop staring at my feet; you're making this weird."

Shit, he noticed. My face heated as I nodded and barreled out of the room. I couldn't even look him in the eyes now that he'd caught me eye-fucking his toes. "Get it together, Eden," I reprimanded myself, not paying the least bit of attention to my surroundings while I headed upstairs in search of someone that could tell me where I'd be staying and where my shit was, not that I would be complaining if I needed to bunk with Santos. I got the gist that he didn't want me around, not while he was indisposed anyway, so I was on my own to figure shit out. Nothing new there, but it would have been much easier if I could just text or call one of the others. There was no way I was going back for my purse right now. I'd just have to roam the halls until a Carlotti popped up; they were bound to be around here somewhere. Before I left, I could barely take a step without tripping over one of them.

As if I'd summoned him, Tony appeared around the corner, presumably coming from his office. He froze in his tracks when his eyes met mine, then had much the same reaction as Santos.

"Vanni or my father?" he asked, recovering quite a bit faster than his enforcer had. But that was Tony, cold and calculated, while his counterpart ran hot and headstrong. Had I not known they definitely didn't swing that way, I'd have thought they were more than best friends—that old 'opposites attract' theory.

But all that control meant that I couldn't help but fuck with the eldest Carlotti heir. Ruffling his feathers was fun when I knew he wasn't going to off my ass for looking at him sideways. *Hmm...might be that they are more alike than I thought.* "Maybe I missed your grouchy ass? Ever think of that?"

Completely ignoring me, he went on with his stick-up-the-ass routine. One of these days, I was gonna yank it out and beat him with it. Then give Santos a few whacks for good measure too. "Eden, I'm serious. It's not safe for you here right now. You weren't supposed to come back until the situation was handled." He already had his phone out, thumbs flying across the keyboard before he'd even finished speaking. I started to give him the same reasoning I'd given Santos, but then confusion set in.

"Wait, if you didn't know I was coming, then where the fuck are my bags? The attorneys said someone was picking up the car and bringing it back here. I'm not wearing Marco's fucking clothes again."

I didn't get an answer from Tony, though, if he was even going to deign to give me one. "Aww, I knew I heard my Lady Garden." Marco's voice came from behind me right as his arms snaked around me, causing me to jump in reaction. The fucker was silent on his big ass feet, and I had to battle with the heart attack he'd tried to give me before I could relax into his hold. But the tingles he elicited as his warm breath hit my ear quickly directed my focus a bit farther south of my chest, doing nothing to calm my racing pulse. "I'm hurt, though. I thought you liked getting in my pants."

"I knew one of you had to miss me too," I managed, not at all sounding like I'd be happy for him to drag me off and deal with the rest later. I really had missed them, and now three of the four were accounted for. My desire to find Vanni battled with my need to stay right where I was...in Marco's arms.

He seemed to have at least half of the same thoughts as he didn't waste any time, spinning me and gripping the backs of my thighs in his big hands before picking me up and pinning me to the wall with his hips. Tony's "Marco, not now!" was drowned out as Marco's face filled my vision. His scent enveloped me, urging me to taste the man that drove me crazy in all the best ways.

"Of course I missed you," he breathed against my lips before darting his tongue out to lick them like he couldn't help but need to taste me. "I missed you before you left, and every day since then. We all did. Don't let those fuckers try to tell you differently."

Hazel orbs fixed on me in a determined stare, Marco continued to ignore Tony while we existed in our own little bubble. I desperately wanted him to kiss me. I could close the miniscule space between us and do it myself, but I felt the need to be chased and caught instead of feeling like a case of convenience. I needed him to prove his words with actions to back them up. I just *needed*.

Hands leaving where they'd been resting on my hips, one smacked the wall next to my head while the other curled into a loose fist to trail the backs of his knuckles across my cheek. The soft and tentative caress matched the suddenly vulnerable look he now wore. "You're never leaving us again, Edie, promise. I don't care who says what. You fight to stay, and I'll fight to keep you. Deal?"

There's only one answer I can give him. My "Deal" barely leaves my lips before his are on mine, insistent and possessive as fuck, demanding and begging all at once. The carnal kiss held the answers I sought—when I got him alone, he was going to give me more than the fucking tip this time. I'd have told him so, but the moment only became more heated, and the appendage in question hardened against me.

Then something I hadn't yet had the fortune of experiencing happened. His dick was pressed right up against my now healed piercings, hitting them just right through the thin layers of leggings and panties. The pressure made my pussy clench hard on absolutely nothing, just as hard as my hands gripped his shoulders. It had taken a bit to get used to my pants rubbing on them, and I got turned on a lot, but this was in another league altogether. If he kept it up, I'd come without him doing a damned thing else.

A moan ripped from my throat despite my intent to keep quiet, and I wrapped my legs tightly around his waist, arching against him in response. I broke the kiss as my head tipped back, banging against the wall, my eyes barely slitted enough to see the mix of heated bewilderment on Marco's face as he quirked a brow and took in my extremely aroused state. His attention traveled from my now messy ponytail to settle on my hardened nipples showing plainly through my bra and shirt.

Experimentally, he flexed his hips, hoisting me further up, so I settled better atop him before rotating to rub his erection hard against my center. A few more concentrated grinding motions and I panted through my orgasm, completely blindsided by the intensity that little bit of hardware had delivered. "Oh, fuck, Marco, you have to stop. I can't take any more," I finally pleaded as the devilish man rocked against me, a smug ass smirk pulling up one side of his plush lips that still bore a slight swollen redness from our encounter. I was sure it matched my own, but all I really cared about at the moment was the fact that he stopped. Not to mention I wasn't sure I could actually feel my legs.

"I think Edie has some explaining to do," he stated. His eyes were no longer quite so smug, holding a definite hint of flinty steel. "Who were you pre-gaming with? And fair warning, if it wasn't Santos, I'll be breaking the terms of my house arrest."

My eyes cut to the side, seeking anything to avoid explaining my new accessories. I wasn't hiding them, but it didn't seem like the thing one should just blurt out when one wasn't quite sure how to explain that they'd missed all of them and had gotten piercings to match their ex when said ex didn't know about it yet. It really was a whole damned *thing* I'd built up in my head. Plus, I sorta liked the whole jealous-possessive thing Marco had going on at the moment. Until my gaze landed on a narrow-eyed Tony, who I couldn't help but notice had a definite tent in his pants even though it looked like he'd tried to tuck it up to make it less noticeable, not that he'd managed it. At all. Then my lack of inhibition had me all sorts of embarrassed; I'd just dry-humped Marco until I got off. In the middle of the hallway...while Tony watched.

"Antonio." I greeted him as if we hadn't been in the middle of a conversation before Marco interrupted; my smooth self even gave him a little nod like

I wasn't still wrapped around his cousin and pinned against his wall.

With a smirk I thought he tried to hide, Tony tipped his head at me in return. "Eden." *Is Antonio Carlotti actually playing along?* I was pleasantly surprised by the turn of events, not that I got to revel in it for more than a second or two. Marco had decided to be persistent in his pursuit of answers. Namely, if I'd been screwing around with anyone.

"Edie, if anyone else has been touching what's mine—"

"*Ours*," Tony interjected, resulting in my attention snapping directly back to him. I stared, wide-eyed, not daring to hope he meant it while simultaneously wanting to demand he say it again.

"Yes, ours, we get it, Tony. What I don't get is how I'm standing here with a wet patch on my jeans, still hard as fuck, while Edie here is already done and also in need of a change of clothes." Right about then, Marco wedged fingers between us to prove his point and found my surprise. I wasn't the only one wide-eyed thanks to new developments, and Marco's crooked smile soon bloomed with a renewed heat between my legs as he manipulated the rings with his fingertips.

My sharp intake of air was drowned out by a crash from downstairs and Santos' raised voice. We all froze for an instant before Tony dashed past us. Marco let my legs down, barely checking that I was steady before he took off to investigate the commotion. The whiplash of one event crashing into the next was beginning to wear on me, but really, it was par for the course in my life. My all-too-short reprieve from it had been nice, but I supposed it was time to get back to the real world.

four

don't be shy

Eden

"**I** said get the fuck out!" Santos was still yelling at the nurse while hanging on to his IV pole like it was a crutch. Tony was advancing on the poor woman, apparently not even bothering to find out why Santos was having a hissy. But the way Santos' clothes hung on him caught my attention, and it was enough to distract me from the room's other occupants. He'd lost weight.

I hadn't noticed it earlier, but his cheekbones were definitely a bit sharper now that I looked for it. It wasn't a ton, but I was fairly certain the t-shirt he had on was supposed to be fitted, not loose. Guilt flared at my earlier inattention as I studied him while trying to avoid him thinking I was staring at his scars. My focus had been zeroed in on what he had underneath the bandage and if the other guys were okay, and not much else.

"What the fuck is going on in here?" came from behind me, directly followed up with, "Eden? When did you get back, and more importantly, *why* are you here?" *Isn't that the question of the day?* The voice the question came from happened to be attached to my missing Carlotti, and I twisted to find Vanni, who was irritated as fuck, all the way from his pinched brows to his scowling lips. I didn't miss the weight loss this time; Vanni was straight-up gaunt, with dark circles under his eyes. I didn't see any visible injuries, but I would be finding out as soon as Santos' issue with his nurse was resolved.

"Hey, Vanni. Yes, I'm back, and also...you look like shit, but you could still give me a hug or try to act like you're happy to see me. Ya know, the person that came all this way to say you didn't off me and bury me in the backyard or some shit like that?" His lack of reaction bugged me. He just continued to stare until I felt awkward as fuck and edged away from him. "Right, so you're *not* happy to see me. Got it." Feeling that burn of embarrassment and hurt, I pretended not to care, tuning into what Tony and Santos were arguing about. The nurse stood off to the side, looking exactly like I felt, and a bit of sympathy went out to her. I knew exactly how hard it was to deal with this bunch.

"A few days until Doc clears you, Santos. You can't put up with help until then? It's what's keeping your stubborn ass out of the hospital, and you know it. Otherwise, you would have been left there." Tony's low tone wasn't enough to keep his words private in the quiet room, but I doubted he cared too much, or he'd have already kicked everyone out.

"He's clearing me tomorrow, so it's a non-issue," Santos snarled back, posturing like he didn't have a care in the world. Except the sweat beading up on his forehead, dampening his hairline, gave away just how much it was costing him to put up the front.

Begin as you plan to continue. As Tony continued to argue that he was *maybe* getting cleared tomorrow, I decided to take matters into my own hands. Shooting a glance at Marco, who was leaning against the wall like it was his job to hold it up, to see if he was going to try to stop me, I approached the duo.

"Tony, take care of the nurse. Get any instructions I'll need to know and put her somewhere out of the way but near enough that she can come in an emergency. Santos, get your ass back in that bed before you fall on it." I wasn't certain they'd follow along, and I was going to look like a complete fool if they didn't, but after a long, indecipherable look from Tony, he nodded and moved to escort the woman out.

"She'll be in the next room over if you need her," he said to me before narrowing his eyes on Santos. "Give Eden shit, and I'll take you back to the hospital myself."

With that warning, he left, the nurse in tow, and I took charge of Santos. Or tried to. His legs had apparently had enough of his shit, too, and were threatening to give out. Trying not to hurt him, I quickly moved to get under his arm on his bad side. Thankfully, he didn't let up with his white-knuckled grip on the pole, so I didn't have too much of his weight to handle. Done with his wall-holding duty, Marco was next to me in an instant, getting behind Santos. He helped me get him the couple steps to the bed, the two of us lowering him without jarring his injuries. I nearly ended up underneath him, and all sorts of thoughts and feelings hit me. I hadn't been in a bed with Santos in so long that I wasn't quite sure what to do except bolt. But that wasn't quite an option after boldly proclaiming that I'd step in as nursemaid. I didn't regret the offer, but that didn't mean I wouldn't soon enough if this was my reaction. My plans hadn't made it much past getting back and refusing to let them ship me off again, and now I was sort of regretting my lack of preparation.

Marco seemed to pick up on my discomfort as he helped Santos get situated with a wink in my direction, but then, of course he opened his fat mouth. "Now that we're alone, did you know Edie has something she wants to share?"

"Marco," I hissed, mortified that he'd even think about it, "that's not appropriate. And I will smother you in your sleep if you don't shut your trap right now!" With a grin, the asshole mimed zipping his lips, but from the devilry dancing in his eyes, I knew it wouldn't keep him quiet for long. I turned to straighten the blanket, using the maneuver as cover to regain my composure, and noticed Vanni was gone. His absence was enough to sober me up, making me wonder what the fuck his problem was, not that I felt I had any right to go ask him after the reception he'd given me.

"Fine, take all the fun out of it, you shrew," Marco teased, but when I looked up at him, he had his attention on the empty doorway as well, and the jovial tone didn't match the worry in his stare.

Needing some semblance of order, I focused on the one thing that actually required my attention—Santos' care. "Is there anything you need right now?" I asked the man in question. His head shake and crossed arms didn't bode well for us getting along, and I had an inkling that I'd be turning the nursing duties back over to the actual professional very soon. With that in mind, I figured I'd be better off finding out what had him kicking her out in the first place.

"What did she do that was so awful, anyway? Try to hold your dick while you took a piss?" I was being a smartass, but when he remained silent, I had to raise my brows in surprise. "Really? Huh, I could have gotten paid a lot more if I'd known my skill as a professional dick holder was a legitimate job description."

Santos coughed like he'd choked on his spit before grimacing in pain and glaring at me while Marco tried to impersonate a hyena. That familiar burn of embarrassment crept up once again as they both regained their composure. *One day I won't pop off with remarks that show exactly how far in the gutter I lived.* Unfortunately, that wasn't today.

With a sigh, I propped my hands on my hips and glared at Marco. "Keep it up, asshole, and these hands won't go near your pecker again."

That sobered him up, but it pissed Santos off.

"Excuse me? What'd you do, go straight upstairs to fuck?" He seemed to regret his outburst as soon as he said it, but he wasn't the only one pissed off now.

"Santos, don't talk to her like that. You're being a jealous ass. As usual," Marco tacked on, making me wonder if this had been a *thing* while I was gone.

I couldn't find my footing since I got back to town, and none of this indicated that would happen anytime soon. I'd thought when I left, that things would be different when I returned, but now I was sort of regretting not taking off again after going to the police station.

Mad and a little bit sad, I stuck up for myself. "It doesn't matter what I do with my own time or body, Santos. We're not together, remember? I don't know why I bothered to try. I'll let the nurse know she still needs to put up with your contrary self until Doc gives you the all-clear."

I turned on my heel, intent on finding Tony to deliver the news then chasing down my damn clothes and where I'd be staying. My wet underwear was starting to chafe, and I wanted them off.

"Eden, wait. I didn't mean it like that! You just took me by surprise. You barely left here, and..." He mashed his lips into a firm line as I turned my head over my shoulder to give him my attention, but he didn't finish whatever he had planned to say. Instead, he flicked his gaze to Marco and glared some more. I *so* wasn't putting up with his crap or his fake apologies.

Of course, I couldn't even make it out of the room before Tony came back with Vanni in tow. One look from me to the men behind me, and Tony's sigh could be heard all the way upstairs. "What now? How could you have pissed her off in the few minutes I've been gone, Santos? Her presence is what allowed Doc to let you recuperate at home, and you're damn well aware of it!" Apparently, I wasn't the only one fed up with his bullshit.

"If he actually needs help, let me know. Princess over there took offense to the nurse trying to touch him in his no-no square while doing her job." My eyes nearly rolled hard enough to sprain something, but the lack of response and the frozen Carlottis in front of me clued me in that I'd hit on a major faux pas. "What?" I asked, swiveling my head to look back at Santos and Marco, but their attention wasn't on me. They were staring past me at Tony and Vanni.

"I'm going to go check the, uh, something. I'll be back later." And with that stuttered declaration, Vanni disappeared from the doorway.

In my confusion, the only thing I could imagine was that they *were* screwing someone else. It was a harsh blow, one I'd expected before, well, everything that had happened, but not now.

"I didn't mean to intrude," I started, wanting nothing more than to escape with whatever dignity I had left. And find someone to fix the fucking tattoo asap. "I would have stayed gone had I known..." Lifting my hand to gesture to all of them, I made myself walk toward Tony, hoping he'd move out of the way without making this a thing. I knew damn well I could have gone to any police station and declared myself fine. I hadn't had to risk coming back here, but I'd wanted to, and Vinnie had asked, no, nearly *demanded* my presence. *Something he hadn't discussed with them beforehand.* Either Vinnie didn't know, or he didn't want *me* to know. I wasn't supposed to be here; that was the consensus.

Except that didn't explain Marco's actions or Tony's remark upstairs. I'd thought he meant 'ours' as in all four, or maybe he'd literally meant the two of them. But Tony hadn't tried to touch me either, only Marco had, and I had to consider that the "ours" could be more in the Family sense rather than the personal relationship sense that I'd stupidly assumed. *What the fuck is going on?*

In desperate need of redirection, I latched on to the first thing that popped in my head. "I need to speak to Vinnie, and then I'll get my things and go." *Yeah, go talk to Vinnie with the crotch of your pants soaked. That's going to be fun.* But I didn't know what else to do. I had no idea where my things were.

"You're not fucking leaving. Just calm the fuck down for a minute and explain what you think you know," Tony ordered, moving more fully into the doorway to block my exit. I barely stopped quickly enough to keep from plastering myself against his chest.

"Antonio, I've had enough for today. Please let me pass." I wasn't going to fucking cry in front of them, that just wasn't me, but my voice wasn't as strong as it could have been, and I couldn't force myself to look up and make eye contact. *So much for beginning as I planned to continue.* Fuck, I felt stupid.

"No," was what I got in return, but not from Tony. Heavily tattooed arms came around me, one sporting a port with tubing attached, and pulled me back against a solid chest. Underneath the antiseptic, his scent was much the same as it had always been, and I nearly panicked at the prickle behind my eyes. They weren't playing fair. I couldn't take this shit, but with the thought of the bandage across his side and back, I also didn't want to struggle and possibly hurt him.

"You're supposed to be in bed, Santos," I managed, albeit a bit on the shaky side.

"Fuck the bed. I told you I don't need help. That woman is just too scared to *not* offer assistance, and she's interested enough in the Carlotti name to even try for *me*." I hated the way he said it, like he didn't matter, and I despised my weak ass for caring. The man was unreliable and could hold a grudge 'til the end of time from what I'd gathered. He didn't turn me loose, though, and I was really feeling awkward as fuck between him and Tony.

"Give her a hug, asshole." *Thank you, Marco, for making it so much worse.*

But then Tony closed the scant distance between us, leaning in, while encircling my body around Santos' arms. "You're not leaving, and you're going to sit your ass down and explain." The rough timbre of his voice reverberated in my ear and sent goose-bumps trailing my skin in a wash of erotic sensation. He might be an asshole, but fuck, he flat out did it for me. They all did.

"Alright, you hugged it out. Santos, back to bed, or I'm calling the doc. Tony, help Eden find her clothes and figure out where she's sleeping, prefer-ably in one of our beds if you don't mind. I'm going to try to sort Vanni out." Marco edged around the back of Tony before I could ask what he was talking about, not to mention why he was so damn bossy and didn't get shit on over it.

"Try to take off, angel, and I'll be doing more than breaking Doc's orders," Santos rumbled behind me as he let go and headed back for the bed.

Which left me with Tony, again. "Little room, please, Tony. You're kinda freaking me out. And if you guys aren't hooking up with anyone, then why did Vanni take off?"

He stepped back and shushed Santos, telling him to keep his ass in bed, before pinching the bridge of his nose and bowing his head. "First, we aren't screwing anyone, and we need to have a discussion about that at some point soon. Second, shit went down at the jail. It's how we got released to house arrest, but it's also why the first conversation may have to be put on hold." That was cryptic as fuck, as well a huge relief, but I got sidetracked when posh-ass Tony raised the leg of his pressed slacks to reveal the little black box strapped to his ankle. *Tony fucking Carlotti has an ankle monitor.*

"You all got tethers?" I asked, tone full of disbelief. It made sense, theoretically, but I was surprised their attorneys hadn't found some way to wiggle out of it.

"Yes, which has made handling some details a pain in the ass. Everyone and their fucking dog knows to watch the estate because we can't leave without landing our asses right back in jail, and that isn't an option right now."

Broaching the subject I'd just been roundaboutly told to wait on, I asked about Vanni. "What was Vanni's problem, then? If I'm going to stay here, I need answers, Tony. I'm not a drugged-up whore anymore. I'm not a threat to any of you, and I'm almost fully recovered from my injuries." At Tony's sharp glance and Santos' exclamation at the 'fully' part, I added on, "My ribs are still sore if I put them under too much stress, but it's nothing major. Doc warned me that might happen. I wasn't in the best of health to begin with even though I was a lot better than when you first found me." I paused to glance back at Santos before finishing with a touch of levity. "I'd probably have died in that room, and stayed that way, if the mob boss in training and sidekick hadn't shanghaied my ass."

It earned me a brief hint of a grin from Santos, but he still looked troubled, considering the frown that seemed to be permanently etched on his face settled back into place. With a shrug, I gave Tony my attention again, laughing at the annoyance on his face. But I quickly found out it wasn't all aimed at me.

"You've been summoned to the main house," he bit out, jaw ticking through his cheek. "My father is under the impression that you were delivered here by mistake. Your belongings have been installed in a guest room, where he's informed me you'll be staying for the duration of your visit." His hard gaze flicked from me, to the screen of his phone and back again, suspicion written all over his face, but I was at just as much of a loss.

"Visit? That implies you're leaving, Eden, and I just told you that you aren't. Tony, take care of it, or I'm going up there myself. We aren't children to be managed; he's all but handed all the operations over." Santos' fury was evident in his voice, and I didn't have the heart to tell him I'd agreed to follow Vinnie's lead to help get them out of this mess.

I hadn't known he'd want to keep me away from them, and a sense of betrayal welled up in me that his intent had been to use me all along, but I fought to push it back down. I wouldn't jump to any conclusions, at least not before I had a chance to get my questions answered. "Guess I'll head up there and see what he wants," I informed them on a sigh. Then another thought occurred. "Can you even go that far with the tethers?" From Tony's scowl and Santos' grunt, I took that as a no. "Well then, can I borrow a car?"

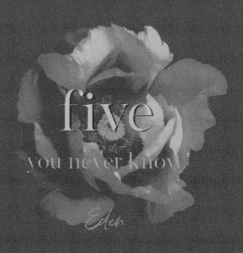

five

you never know

Eden

He can't be serious...

Fingers steepled, elbows on the top of his pristine desk, and dark eyes focused on me in a hard stare, Vinnie reiterated his last question when I couldn't quite find my voice. "Miss Moretti, do you understand what I'm asking of you?"

Oh, I sure as fuck did, and if he was asking, I was a fucking monkey named George. Either way, I was screwed, blued, and tattooed. And in my case, with the cumulative events since I'd crash-landed back in the vicinity of the Carlottis, it was fairly literal. But after what I'd just learned...

"Yes," I replied as tonelessly as possible while holding on to my composure by the skin of my fucking teeth.

He sighed like *he* was the one put out. "I do sympathize with you over the position you're in, but you did offer your assistance when you reached out. You had the choice of staying out of the situation." Thinking he was done, I was going to ask to be excused, but just as I made to lift up a little, the hardened mafia don mien cracked. He briefly let his rage and hurt show before smoothing it back out. "There aren't rules of engagement in our world, yet you reap what you sow. Rodrigo went too far when he had my sons and nephew attacked." It wasn't lost on me that he left Santos out, and I had to wonder if he blamed Santos for not protecting his blood, injured or not. I watched as he paused and swallowed, and then, without meeting my eyes, which I was grateful for as I had my own trouble dealing with it, he finished. "After what was done to Giovanni... It will be the complete annihilation of every last one of those fucks that planned, knew about, or touched my son."

And that right there was why I couldn't tell him to screw off and leave town again. Why I would have to keep my plans, and Vinnie's, from the guys until it was over. Then, maybe, we could all have a shot at something real—if I didn't wind up dead first. And that brought me to the one stipulation that I wasn't going to abide by.

"I'm staying at the guest house until I'm needed. They're going to ask questions already, and they'll probably resort to doing something they shouldn't if I'm suddenly here instead of there." I almost said Santos would come up here, but I didn't think he was Vinnie's favorite person after Rodrigo's defection and Santos' failure to prevent Vanni from being sodomized. It wasn't Santos' fault, and if Vinnie went after him in any way, he'd be facing more than just my retribution. Surely he knew it was a distinct possibility that his eldest son would be the first person to have a go at him if he dared attempt it.

He debated long enough to have me worried he'd deny me even a little time with them, and my palms slicked with sweat that my leggings just couldn't keep up with until he slowly nodded, not a single strand of his salt and pepper hair falling out of place.

"I suppose that would be acceptable as long as you make the proper excuses for your absences." I could almost hear an echo of Tony's voice from that night, nearly the first words he'd said to me in years. *Snitches and ditches, remember?*

"Yes, Mr. Carlotti, I understand." I bit my lip as I stood from the chair in front of his desk, braving one last question. "There will be men there? To watch my back?"

"As I said, you'll be followed, discreetly." That didn't exactly allay my fears, but it would have to do. I wasn't a weak ass bitch that couldn't handle myself, and I needed to remember that fact.

Giving him a plastic smile, the one I used to reserve for customers, I dipped my head in respect. "Of course, I'll be on standby." With a wave of the new phone he'd given me, I headed for the office door.

"Oh, and please, call me Vinnie next time. Such formality isn't needed when you're doing your duty for the Family."

I couldn't turn around; I'd have said something that would have landed my ass in hot water, and it was already hanging out in the breeze after what I'd just agreed to do. Intent on hurrying back to Tony's place, I went in search of my belongings, fully determined to spend every minute I had left with them while I could. When they found out that I'd gone behind their backs, I was afraid they might hate me.

Bags in tow, I clunked up the steps and wrestled with the door, vaguely regretting declining the offer of assistance from one of Vinnie's house staff. As I backed into the entryway, the weight on my shoulder lifted, and I glanced over my shoulder to find Tony pulling the door open for me as he took my bag.

"Here, give me that one, too," he said, gesturing to the large rolling suitcase I was pulling. It felt odd to let him take it all while I was nearly empty-handed, and I debated telling him I had it, but I decided to give in.

"Thanks. I can take the duffel back if you'd like?" It was awkward having nothing in my hands while Tony played bellhop, but he shook his head before collapsing the handle on the suitcase and picking it up like it was nothing.

"You want a room down here or upstairs?"

I didn't know how to answer him. On the one hand, his offer to be upstairs was a giant leap from being locked in the room down here, but it would be easier to leave and do what Vinnie needed if I was closer to the door. "Um, I'm not sure. I thought I'd be getting the same one back, but Santos is in there, and..." I shrugged, not sure where I was going with my own thoughts.

But Tony didn't seem to think it was odd, or if he did, he kept it to himself. He was different, and I suspected it was thanks to their attack in jail. *Would he revert back to being a dick again?* "Santos can't do the stairs yet, and he's been in there being a mopey shit since you left, so I don't think you'd be staying in there alone even if he wasn't in it recovering. I'd feel more comfortable with you upstairs with the rest of us, but it's up to you."

Put that way, I decided to opt for upstairs. I'd just have to figure out how to get away when needed. "With you, all is fine."

Satisfaction lit his stare before he turned to guide me through the house, using the time to interrogate me. "Since my father ignored my calls and messages,

I'm going to assume you made some sort of deal to come back here?"

The truth wasn't an option, so even though there was a hint of regret for the lies I was about to hand him, I blithely delivered them anyway. "He thought I was only coming back to prove I was alive and well, then leaving again. When I let him know I was going to be sticking around for a while, he had my things brought down. Your car and the one I've been using are both in the garage, by the way."

"Yes, I'm aware, and the car is yours. I'll have it transferred into your name as soon as you renew your license. The only reason it wasn't before is so that it wasn't linked to you. It's currently under a rental company, but it shouldn't take long once the paperwork is filed."

"You don't have to do that, Tony—" I started to protest, but he cut me off.

"I want to. Hell, the others will if I don't, so you're stuck with it. Unless you want something else?"

"No, it's a great car. Thank you." I swore he was dragging his feet, going as slowly as possible to make this conversation even more awkward. Talking to him had never been easy, but this was painful. And he fucking stopped mid-way up the damn stairs to pin me in place with narrowed eyes.

"Want to tell me what was *really* discussed up at the house? I'm not buying that my father wanted to protect your delicate sensibilities from us. He likes you well enough, but he wouldn't intervene that way."

Oh, if only you knew how very far he's into your business, buddy. "He wanted to keep an eye on me and make sure I wasn't blinding you with my golden pussy." Rolling my eyes for effect, I gestured for him to move along, and thankfully, he did, albeit with a grunt of annoyance or maybe disbelief.

"I'll take that answer for now. I wouldn't have put it past you before, so I can see where he'd think that," he popped off like it didn't bug me in the slightest for him to think I was so cutthroat. I mean, he wouldn't be wrong, but still, it wasn't polite to bring it up *now*. To top it off, we were going right by the scene where my panties were murdered in broad daylight. It was like that murder mystery game, only the adult version. 'Marco Carlotti committed the crime in the upstairs hallway with a boner and a hood ornament.' Of course, the dick's cousin had to bring it up, too. "What was that all about? You know it's not nice to play with him if you're not going to stay."

It was my turn to grunt, and fuck it if it wasn't ladylike. We passed closed bedrooms, all silent except for Marco's music thumping away behind his door, while I debated what to say. As we came to an open, unoccupied room, I finally answered him, voice tart with being put on the spot about it. Not to mention that I still desperately needed to change my clothes and was kinda cranky about it. "Apparently, I went and caught feels despite my sense of self-preservation telling me not to."

At my candid response, Tony nearly fell through the door he was pushing open, but he quickly caught himself as he muttered, "Yeah, and it was contagious."

I couldn't hold in a laugh at the consternation on his face when he did the gentlemanly thing and held the door for me. I patted his cheek as I edged by him and my suitcase. "It's definitely an adjustment for sure, but I can't say I'm disappointed that you were struck with the same illness." I winked and gave him a shrug when I seemed to take him off guard again. If the future wasn't so uncertain, I'd be a bit more hesitant, but fuck if I knew when Vinnie was going to tag me in on his scheme. I didn't have any time to waste.

"Take it easy on Santos...and Vanni too. They're not quite up to your new... whatever this is." He waved his hand up and down at me, probably at a loss for a description that wouldn't threaten the state of his balls. My frown was immediate, but not at him, and he seemed to clue in on that. "Ah, so he did tell you," he said, referencing Vinnie, though that only made me nervous that I was about to be blamed and in deep shit for Tony finding out after I'd been told to keep my mouth shut. "Don't think I don't know my father is up to something. He wouldn't be in his position if he were a man without strategy. But know this, if whatever he's cooked up makes me lose any of you, there's going to be hell to pay."

It was much the same thought I'd already had, and a lump full of trepidation lodged in my throat until all I could do was nod that I understood him, but at least he didn't know the extent of what his father had in store for me. "I'll leave these here and let you settle in. Let me know if you need anything." Another nod from me, and he turned to go. Immediately, he doubled back with a "Fuck, it," pulling me in to brush his lips against my forehead before leaving and shutting the door behind him. I touched my fingertips to my lips as I stared at the door, my heart torn in two at the necessity of going behind their backs to protect them and the betrayal they would feel if shit didn't go as planned.

In my experience, Eden Moretti didn't have much of a lucky streak in her...

six

i love you

Eden

As I unpacked, I surveyed the very...plain room. Off-white and light gray was the extent of the color scheme. It had twin nightstands, a dresser, a desk and chair, and a decent-sized walk-in closet. The attached bathroom wasn't quite as opulent as the one downstairs, but it still wasn't anything to sneeze at. Not to mention, it was an Empire State Building's worth of a step up from my old apartment. I took advantage of the seemingly endless hot water before I went to find out what was happening for dinner.

My long hair hung in damp, loose waves, and I was once again in leggings, topped with a slouchy sweater over a tank top, and bare feet as I went in search of food. An off-key humming caught my attention as I got closer to the kitchen, the sound growing louder when I pushed open the doors, startling Vanni. He looked hot and very domestic in his dark jeans and apron-covered t-shirt as he spun to face me, tension pinching the corners of his eyes and lips. He relaxed when he saw it was just me, but it was too late for the pieces of asparagus he'd been snapping at the sink. In his haste to turn around, they'd gone flying to parts unknown.

"Did you see where they went?" It took me a second to realize that he meant the ends and not that he was looking for someone. I made a cursory sweep of the floor, but I was more interested in Vanni, wondering if he was going to run off again. He must have mistaken my attention and silence as something else than the wait-and-see that it was. Tone filled with disdain, he let me know exactly how he felt about it too. "Guess you were filled in on everything?" Before I could try to figure out what to say, which shouldn't have been hard considering I'd been in his shoes more than once, he curled his lips into a disgusted sneer. "I don't need *your* fucking pity too, Edie! I get enough of that shit from my brother and Santos."

Apparently done with me, he threw the handful of stalks he still held back into the colander in the sink and started hunting for the pieces he'd lost. I wasn't sure that they were all that important; I thought it was more about it being something he could control. Not that I was about to bring that up, given his already precarious mood. So I started helping, taking one side of the kitchen, as far away as I could get to give him some space, and worked my way in.

"I don't pity you, Vanni. Feel bad, sure, but I'm positive you felt bad about me, too. Unless you pitied me? I understand if you did. I was kind of pathetic and an easy target. Hell, I probably still am, considering the way the others demanded to know why I was back." He made a few noncommittal hums, and I refused to look up.

The damn asparagus must have grown legs and walked off from all the luck we had at finding it until we both spied one under the edge of the refrigerator. We didn't bump heads, but the bob and weave could have doubled for slap-stick comedy, well, a bad one, maybe. But at least it got a reaction out of Vanni.

"Motherfucker," he barked out on a laugh. "You get it before we end up knocking each other on the floor, looking like a pair of idiots." He stood there, hands on his hips as I knelt down to fish the green stem from its hidey-hole, but neither of us were laughing after I glanced back up and realized we were in a very déjà vu sort of situation. Eyes wide, not quite with panic but more a mix of heat and embarrassed dismay. "I-I, uh, shit. I didn't think...fuck my life. Can you just get up?" he finally spat with his eyes closed and fists clenched.

The old me would have taken advantage to get the upper hand, and maybe he was having the same thoughts because that's exactly what I *had* done the last time I'd been on my knees before him in this kitchen. Yet I couldn't let it go. I didn't know if that made me a shitty person, or insensitive, or whatever, but this felt like one of those points in life where if you made the wrong decision, it would haunt you for a very, very long time.

"No." The simple refusal was delivered with a level of calm I definitely wasn't feeling, but it had the desired effect of snapping him out of his flustered state.

"What do you mean, *no*, Eden? You know I wasn't propositioning you, right?" A muscle in his cheek ticced as he clenched his jaw as tightly as his fists.

"Never said you were. You're the one that got all weird about it instead of cracking a joke and laughing it off. Kinda makes me think that's *exactly* what you wanted to do." My shrug just seemed to piss him off more, and I worried I'd pushed him too far, but he'd said he didn't want my pity. I wasn't about to start treating him any differently unless he told me to back off.

"We treated you like shit, fucked with you despite knowing what you'd been through. Hell, we pretty much gangbanged your ass and acted like it was just fine. Why would you be interested in any of us at all? You know you don't have to do *that* for us to take care of you, right?" The genuine concern and guilt in voice and eyes threw me a bit. I knew they all regretted being assholes to me, and the parts they'd played in my life going to shit, however inadvertently it had been, but it was pretty clear they wanted to make up for it all. Vanni had even offered to go behind all of their backs to help me disappear for good if that was what I wanted, so he was the last person I'd have expected to say any of that. Besides, Marco had been a fucking saint compared to the rest of them, yet Vanni still lumped him in with all of them. *What the fuck else happened while I was gone?* I tried to feel my way around whatever was happening right then without making this twitchy, pissed-off version of Vanni spook and run again like he had earlier.

"So you didn't pity me before, or at least not for long, but now you do? And you think I'm whoring myself out for...what, exactly?" I wasn't mad since he wasn't completely wrong, but he wasn't quite right either.

"It's not pity; it's regret. We should have treated you better, protected you better." He ran a hand through his dark hair, making it stand on end before it fell into a wayward mess that suited him as much as when he styled it. "Fuck, Edie, we should have been better all around. And here I am, standing around, acting like I can think of anything but my guilt when all I can see in my mind is your lips wrapped around my dick. It's seriously fucking with my head." Of course, I had to break eye contact to check if said dick had the same ideas. I hadn't planned on giving him a blowie, but I wasn't exactly opposed to it.

"You know, I think we've all made enough mistakes and have enough regrets to haunt us. There's no point in dwelling on what we can't change. Personally, I plan to take whatever bit of happiness and pleasure I can get because you never know when life's septic tank is gonna overflow and fuck everything up. It's happened to me more often than I care to admit. I seem doomed to be forever wading through a cesspool with only a bit of dry land here and there to convince me to keep going." Not sure that was the best analogy, but details and getting bogged down in my past weren't what I was after.

"Is that how you move on? How you can act like none of it fazes you? I thought you were too jaded or something, the way you'd crack a joke or be a smartass, but it's the way you deal with it. Make fun of it, detach yourself, and then no one can use it against you." Vanni grew thoughtful at the end of his little revelation/epiphany, enough to not notice he was treading dangerously close to thin ice. I only had so much patience and didn't care to be put on the spot like that. Nor did I want to encourage him to use my questionable coping skills; they weren't exactly healthy.

"Yes, I'm crass and flippant, and people don't

fuck with other people when they're abrasive enough to take a chunk out of your hide just by getting too close. This isn't about me, though; it's about you. If you want your dick sucked, then say so, or don't if you're too polite to bring it up, but whatever weird shit *that* was..." I waved a hand at him, at a loss for what to say that wasn't epically nasty. "Isn't necessary. Not with me anyway."

His jaw worked open and closed as he started and stopped a few times before looking me up and down, trying to gauge if I was serious, I imagined, although I suspected it was a search for more than just simple sincerity.

"Fine." He blew out a breath and worked up a fuck-boy-eqsue expression that reminded me more of Marco than himself, but most importantly, a challenging light lit his gaze as he delivered a seriously juvenile pick-up line. "So, while you're down there..."

An involuntarily snicker escaped me as I remembered him and Marco teasing each other that way for months when we were younger. Anytime one managed to catch the other with their head hip-high or lower, it popped out of the other's mouth. Santos had threatened to beat their asses if they tried it on me, and I wondered if Vanni had done it on purpose to remind us both of better times, that we weren't always piles of fucked up rubble.

As if he couldn't hold a straight face, Vanni's lips curled into a smile, and he hooked his thumbs into the waistband of his pants, prepared to pop the button open at a moment's notice.

"I'm serious, Eden. If you're playing games, now's the time to back off. We'll just forget this happened, and you can help me cook dinner." His tone held a hard edge, punctuating the warning, but I tended to ignore those as a general rule, and this time wasn't any different.

I let my actions speak for me. Instead of my words, I settled more comfortably on my knees. Shaking my hair back out of my face, I reached out a hand to cup the hardening evidence of his desire straining behind the zipper of his jeans.

Vanni just groaned and held my gaze, then his dipped to my lips as I licked them in anticipation of him releasing his thick length, more than ready for him to slip between them.

And then the button slipped out of its hole, and the rasp of his zipper vied for supremacy against the sound of my pulse in my ears. Vanni was going to whip his dick out in the kitchen, knowing anyone could walk in at any time, and prove he could still take exactly what he wanted. Pity didn't exist here, not between us.

"Can I choke you on my dick, Eden? Will you enjoy it if I do?" he asked, voice husky with the desire he'd given in to, then did a complete about-face as if he needed to double and triple-check everything. "Or will it put you back there, when you really had no choice?"

He hesitated with his hand in his boxer briefs, just the tip of his ruddy erection peeking out. I had to consciously lift my attention from it to look up at him and make him understand that right then, I didn't give a fuck about what had happened in the past.

"You have to know I want you as much as I hope that you want me, and I rather like sucking dick when it's not forced on me, Vanni. I kinda get off on it." I shrugged, completely unapologetic for voicing my enjoyment on the subject. I'd leave out not quite caring for the humiliation aspect he'd served up in this very kitchen, but I'd kinda asked for it, so I wouldn't fault him for it. "We never know how long we have. I have every intention of taking whatever pleasure life has to offer with both hands and refusing to let go until I have no other choice." His brows dipped in confusion at my cryptic words, but I headed him off before he could ask more questions. "Give me the D, Vanni. You're leaving me hanging here." I pouted, further drawing his attention from the vague warning that shit might not work out, but also...not a lie. He *was* sort of leaving me hanging there, and my knees couldn't take the position all night.

It was the kick he needed to get things moving. His prick sprung out, loud and proud to be free, perfectly wet at the tip as if it remembered me. I nearly giggled at the thought, but that probably would have been about the worst thing I could have done at that moment, so I swallowed my remark and then Vanni's dick when he pushed his jeans and underwear halfway down his thighs a few seconds later. From the first few teasing licks around the head of his dick, through my eyes watering when I let him slide down my throat, I kept my eyes on his, refusing to let him shy away from me.

"Fuck, Edie, I'm not going to last long with you doing that," he murmured as he held himself rigidly in check. But I didn't want him holding back; he'd said it before, and proved it—he wasn't a gentleman.

I hummed around the crown of his dick where it pressed at the back of my throat before reaching up to grip his asscheeks with both hands, but I stopped everything when he clenched them, flinching away. Letting his member slide out of my mouth, I narrowed my eyes on his. Eyes that weren't quite so lust-filled now.

"Take what you need, Vanni, and tell me if I'm overstepping." I didn't know how else to tell him to take his power back without plainly voicing that he'd been victimized, and that wasn't conducive to current events at all. "I'm not going to break if you're rough, but I'm certain that you already know that."

Scowling down at me, cock losing some of its

rigidity, he shot back, "Is that what you did? Took what you needed and fuck everybody else?"

I tipped my head from side to side, considering his question. "Eh, yes and no. I didn't really have a choice but to own it; it's what I had to do to survive in my situation. Also, I found chemical support fixed just about anything I was feeling and let me coast through everything in a blissed-out numbness." Quietly, I ventured to add another fact to that. "I still miss it sometimes. Not having to feel it all."

His expression went from curious to stricken in an instant, and he completely lost his erection. This was *so* not how I'd planned this going.

"Are you using again? You need drugs to deal with us or your feelings for us? I thought you wanted to be here!" His questions tumbled out rapid-fire, and I groaned at his misunderstanding.

"Jesus, Vanni, no, on all accounts except that last one. I just meant that being a fucked up addict sometimes meant I didn't have to face *or* deal with any of it. If you hadn't noticed, I'm not exactly the poster child for being well-adjusted."

His sigh of relief was echoed by mine, but my leggings weren't up to insulating me from the cold, hard floor, and I was ready to throw in the towel.

"So you *do* want to be here with all of us, and this isn't a pity dick sucking," he stated as if he needed to get it straight in his own head, but I nodded along anyway just to keep things clear. "Well, I cocked this one up then, didn't I?" Rueful laughter tumbled out of me; I couldn't dispute his assertion. Then he let his own tidbit out of the bag, not that I'd been unaware. "I didn't want you to think you couldn't stop if you wanted to, but I really wanted to wrap my hands in your hair and fuck your mouth like no tomorrow."

Even his dick stirred with that statement, and I eyed it, wondering if we were actually going to get back on track. Vanni rubbed the back of his neck with one hand, not at all fazed to be having a heart to heart in the kitchen with his junk hanging out. Sometimes I really envied the brass balls they all sported.

"About the ass grabbing. I know you wouldn't do anything. It was just a reflex..." He trailed off, looking anywhere but at me.

"Vanni, you don't have to be embarrassed or explain why you didn't want me touching you. It's okay."

"But I do. Want you to touch me. I was startled and not expecting it. Can we try again? Unless you'd rather not. I imagine you're getting uncomfortable down there, and I'm starting to feel awkward as fuck, and that's really not my thing."

I had to laugh again but regretted it when his hopeful expression fell. "One day, in the privacy of one of the many bedrooms in this house and not in the middle of the kitchen, I'm going to show you something that will knock your socks off. But only if you agree and *really* trust me. And yes, get your dick hard. This time, do it right."

"I want to fuck you," he declared suddenly, pulling back to wait for my answer.

"Unless you're hiding a condom in those pockets, you're bumming on sex. Besides, I wanted to do this for you. Worry about me later."

"I don't have anything, condom or disease. I was tested. And had to take a bunch of shit just in case. Unless you're not sure you're clean." Oh, he was pissed. I nearly told him to let go of my hair, but I didn't think he noticed he was pulling it. That, and hair pulling didn't bother me. I kinda liked it in the right scenario.

"I'm not on birth control, Giovanni, and I'm not planning on kids anytime soon, nor have I touched anyone besides the four of you since you and Tony picked me up," I snapped back. "Now get to it, or I'm getting up."

"I didn't mean... Goddammit, I'm fucking it all up. I'll make it up to you, yeah?"

Seconds later, his erection was filling back out, and he had my hair fisted in one hand while he fed me his dick with the other. His thrusts weren't as rough as the first time, months ago, but as he fully hardened, I did indeed choke on him a few times.

But I couldn't deny that I was loving it; my pussy got wetter by the second. I was seconds away from daring to take one hand away from his thighs where I'd braced myself to rub one out when the tell-tale pulsing throbbed against my tongue. Vanni pressed as deeply as he could go, negating the need for me to really even swallow by coming directly down my throat. I did need to breathe, though, so I pulled back before he was quite finished, sputtering the last bit of his cum back out. All over his legs.

Well, shit, didn't mean to do that. But Vanni didn't seem to care. He'd barely pulled his pants up on his hips before he grabbed me and moved to the island. He had me laid out, sans bottoms, in five seconds flat, knees hooked over his arms, and then he froze.

"Is that...?"

I decided to own up to it. The man would know soon enough at this rate.

"Yeah, I got them on a whim when I found out there was a chick's version of what Santos has. Also kinda hurt like a bitch while it healed..."

He wasn't looking at me, but he wasn't looking at my crotch either. He was staring directly at the days-old tattoo that was exposed where my shirt had ridden up.

"Huh?" Then his gaze tracked down a bit, and his features went from soft and affectionate to heated and demanding as he reached out to trace a finger over the hoop. "Damn, Edie, you're full of all sorts of surprises. Gonna have to give these a ten out of ten.

And the ink is off the charts." His attention flicked back and forth between the tattoo and piercings before he finally glanced back up at my face. "Don't tell Tony yet. I want to see his face when I tell him I'm first." It took a second, but then I realized he meant the G in GAMES.

"You guys are such adolescents sometimes," I groaned in exasperation, then again for different reasons when he dipped his head to tongue my clit.

"Competitive, there's a difference. Besides, you literally have "The GAMES we play" on your stomach. You have no room to talk, woman." He paused, glancing a bit farther down. "Uh, these are good to go, right? I don't want to hurt you."

"They're fine as long as you don't yank on 'em. I haven't...played with them much yet. And if you quit now, I'm finishing myself off," I threatened.

"No worries, there, Edie. I'll go first again," he declared, smug as fuck and too hot to be legal with his bed head and fuck me dark chocolate eyes. "Try to keep it down, will ya?"

That was all the warning I got before he sucked my clit, rings and all, between his lips, immediately taking up a flicking motion with his tongue. An electric sensation spiraled from my core to my clit and back again before the entirety of the nerve endings between my legs seemed to ignite. The burst of pleasure had me scrabbling for purchase, one hand on the smooth marble top, the other clamping over my mouth to muffle my shriek of ecstasy. I couldn't decide if getting pierced was the best or worst decision I'd ever made as I barreled toward what promised to be an epic orgasm. *How the fuck is it coming so fast?*

Vanni gave me no chance to even attempt to catch my breath, no, the fucker roughly shoved his fingers through my soaked entrance, relentlessly pressing right into the flesh behind my clit. My muscles seized so hard a cramp tightened my abdomen, briefly irritating my tattoo before I felt an embarrassing amount of fluid pulse around the massaging digits my pussy was doing its damnedest to strangle.

"Oh, fuck, Vanni, stop, I can't." My jumbled plea fell on deaf ears as he did just the opposite, then the second wave hit me, eliciting a guttural scream I barely managed to muffle in the crook of my arm. Thankfully, he slowed at that point, but my clit ticked along with my out-of-control pulse like it had its own little heartbeat, a sensation I was afraid wouldn't subside anytime soon.

I lay there, limp and wrung out from the mother of all orgasms, while Vanni gently settled my legs around his waist and wiped his glistening chin on his forearm. *Fuck, I made a mess.* I was sure I'd be embarrassed, maybe, when my scrambled egg brain sorted itself out, but I couldn't even try to complain right now.

Vanni leaned over me, declaring, "Ten out of ten would recommend."

"What?" My brain *so* wasn't back online.

"Kitchen sex, keep up. And also," he said, voice deep and husky with whatever he was feeling, "I fucking love you, Eden Moretti. I'm so glad you came back even if I'd like to spank your ass for taking chances."

Giovanni Carlotti was in love with me. Not. A. Fucking. Lie. It was a damn good thing, too. I'd have had to kill him if he turned me down when I finally got the courage to tell him...even though my ink was likely the catalyst for him fessing up.

He didn't wait for an answer from my shocked self, fusing his lips to mine. The chaste kiss didn't last as he impatiently sought entrance, and quickly enough, our hands tangled in each other's hair just as our tongues did, one gripping tightly while the others swept against each other.

"What the fuck is going on today?" Santos' voice came an instant after the swishing sound of the doors swinging open.

I *did not just fucking hear that.* I could have sworn my ears were playing tricks on me when Vanni's voice filtered through the kitchen doors, declaring for anyone around to hear, and that poor soul happened to be me, that he was in love with Eden.

My Eden.

I hadn't anticipated the scenario I'd walk in on. A month ago, it would have been at the top of my list, but not now. Vanni had Eden sprawled, half-naked, across the kitchen island like he hadn't been avoiding us all since the shit that happened in the jailhouse bathroom, and that would teach me to look through the windows before barging in from now on. But it didn't even feel right to be mad about it, and while a part of me was ecstatic that he wasn't going to let the incident slow him down, feelings weren't always rational.

"Don't look now, Edie," Vanni teased, staring me dead in the eye, mischief written all over his face, "a new player has entered the *game*. Should we tell him he's last?"

"Last *what?*" I didn't like being left out of their inside joke, at all. But neither of them bothered to answer me, and Vanni backtracked to my previous question.

"As for what's going on, well, it seems we need condoms all over this fucking house. Or were you inquiring about dinner? Cuz that's gonna be a bit. I decided to eat my dessert first." With all the snark and self-satisfaction he was radiating, the cocky fuck must have been channeling Marco.

"Vanni, knock it off and give me my pants," Eden admonished before she glanced back at me with a wince.

It pissed me off and hurt me at the same time. She was obviously uncomfortable, or at least self-conscious, about me finding her half-naked and tangled up with Vanni after their tryst. I'd just decided to bow out and go back to bed when a catcalling whistle came from behind me. My groan was instantaneous. Just thinking of the devil had him showing up. All we needed now was for Tony to waltz in and have a coronary over the fact that his kitchen island was *not* being used for its intended purpose. Not that I gave a fuck, but I'd never hear the end of it. The man could hold a grudge like no other.

"Looks like you forgot my invite, assholes. If I'd have known we were playing with Lady Garden's lady garden, I'd have been down here sooner." His grunt of pain immediately followed my elbow connecting with his body. It caused my stitches to pull more than I'd have liked, but I could live with it.

"Marco, shut it. I cannot believe you guys. Vanni, where are my goddamned pants?!" Eden blasted the others even as she sat up and hid her face behind her thick curtain of hair.

It was like I didn't exist to her. My feet shuffled backward as I tried to leave, but Marco refused to move, going so far as to put his hands on my shoulders. I was mobile, but between my exertion and crushing disappointment, I wasn't sure how much longer I was going to be able to stay on my feet. The very last thing I could take right now was looking weak or garnering Eden's pity if I fell on my ass or had to have Marco hold me up.

"Damn, Edie girl, what did Vanni do to you to leave that mess?" He just could not shut up. But as Eden turned to stare in horror, her face flushed from more than just embarrassment, my own gaze landed on the snail trail. And I instantly vowed to never say that in front of her...if I could get her attention for more than guilty glances. A scowl settled firmly on my face at the decent possibility that Eden didn't want shit to do with me despite her concern and letting me hold her earlier.

"You know, this shit was easier to deal with when I didn't care what anyone thought about me," she muttered before pushing Vanni away to stalk to the paper towel holder. Despite her complaints, she was acting completely unfazed that she was still sans pants.

"Let me go, *now*, Marco," I hissed, hoping to avoid drawing attention to my attempt to retreat.

Only he gave it right back, thankfully at a volume that didn't carry over the running sink. Eden was hastily wetting paper towels while letting a kneeling Vanni help her into her pants. "Try not being a chump for five minutes and go sit down. If you let her think this is bothering you, she's going to shut you out. Jesus, it's like you don't know women at all." I could see his head shaking out of the corner of my eye.

He had a point, but I still felt the need to defend myself. "It's not like I have much experience with them, asshole. If you're forgetting, she's the only woman I ever bothered to have a relationship with."

"Also, the only one you ever actually bothered to put your dick in too," he shot back. That just pissed me off even more. Fucking figured he knew I hadn't fucked anyone else. Nosy bastard *always* seemed to know more than his fuckboy persona let on. My inability to get over Eden had been a sore spot until

I'd nearly lost her a second time, and I didn't like that shit being rubbed in my face. Or her being used against me, even by family.

"Don't talk about her like that!" I barely kept from raising my voice, and for the first time since I walked into the kitchen, I was glad Eden was avoiding looking in my direction.

"Then stop being an idiot. That wasn't a slur against Edie, and you know it. Or should we share how we ended up with our hardware?"

"You fucking wouldn't." I'd kick his ass; stitches be damned.

"Wouldn't what?" Oh, *now* she was paying attention. *Motherfucker.*

"Nothing," I snapped, regretting it the instant the word left my mouth when she wilted in front of me. "Marco's just irritating me; it's his specialty," I tried to explain, but she just nodded and went to the fridge for a bottle of water before retreating to the end of the kitchen to lean against the counter. And my legs were telling me to sit the fuck down before they did it for me. On the floor.

As I moved forward, Marco let me go, and I managed to make it to the island, pull a barstool out, and get on it, all without wobbling like a newborn fawn trying to walk for the first time. But that didn't mean he kept his fat ass mouth shut.

"Has Santos told you how he ended up with his dick looking like a bad Pinhead impersonation?" I sighed and glared at Marco as Vanni tried to cover his laugh with a cough.

"Uh, not really," she started, glancing warily between each of us. "Just said he won a bet, right before he shoved them down my throat. Something you all seem rather fond of doing, I might add." Vanni frowned at her, earning an eye roll in return. "I didn't say I didn't like it."

"Well, technically, he won *two* bets," Marco started off, then got whacked with one of the doors when Tony pushed through them.

"Why is everyone in here? This does not look like dinner is being cooked, Giovanni." Tony pointedly stared at his brother, annoyance pinching his features. He quickly made to apologize, as if realizing he'd snapped at his brother, who he'd been treating with kid gloves for days, but Vanni was having none of it.

"I got sidetracked, so it might be best to order in and shush it. Marco was just telling Eden about Santos' strawberry-flavored dick. You might want to stick around to tell your part," he added with a sly grin that had his brother looking him up and down, then over at Eden in speculation.

"*As I was saying*," Marco began again in a huff, "Santos here really won two bets. We all went out to the bar, and after we had a few, I pointed to this chick and told Santos to watch and learn, so maybe he could get a piece... Well, that part isn't important, uh, shit, this is not how I thought this would go." He stumbled over that last part, realizing he'd royally stuck his foot in it.

"Welcome to my world," I muttered, earning wide eyes from Eden. "What Marco is trying to say is that he bet he could hook more women than I could before the night was out. Whoever lost had to get something pierced. I won. The end."

"So then how did you end up with...?" Eden waved her hand in the general direction of my lap.

"That's the second part of it, but you should know he cheated." That was Tony speaking up, much to my utter shock. He usually called us annoying peasants when we started fucking off. Maybe my life-long friend was finally starting to loosen up again. He hadn't been so uptight when we were younger, although that change in him might have had something to do with Eden leaving us like she had. Or, more accurately, like we'd been led to believe. "Santos went and told the women that he was a virgin, and because of a freak accident, he got scarred up, and now Marco was using him as a second-rate wingman. The 'ugly' friend. Once word got around to the ladies in the bar, Marco didn't stand a chance."

It was my turn to wince when Marco turned on me. "You fuck! I knew you couldn't beat me! Goddamned crooks around here. Nice to know you turned on your own cousin, Tony," Marco griped.

Tony just shrugged. "Bros before hoes. You were quite the manwhore about that time if I remember right."

Eden busted out laughing, much to my relief. I'd been half worried that she'd be pissed even though it was years ago, but she was perfectly comfortable with it, and with all of us too, it seemed. Case in point, none of us missed Vanni slipping an arm behind her or the way she relaxed back into him like she belonged there and had done it all of her life.

"Edie, they're being mean to me," Marco complained, trying to garner her sympathy.

"Oh, no. You brought that shit on yourself." She wagged a finger at him like he was a naughty little kid, and even I had to grin at her antics. It was nice to have a light moment in the sea of dark ones that had been accumulating lately. "Okay, so you lost, but Santos is the one that got his dick bedazzled?"

The laughter at my expense was immediate, but all I could do was hold my head and groan. The sooner this shit was over, the better. Wouldn't be so bad if they were fucking with someone else, but I needed to eat and take pain medication, which I didn't want to bring up in front of Eden.

"Yep. We all went in. The others just had to be there to make sure I followed through, then Santos started giving me shit that I was only getting a nipple pierced. Not gonna lie, that shit hurts, in case you were wondering. But you probably know that already, right?" I was at a loss, but from the way Eden glared at him while Vanni hid a smirk, I knew I'd be finding out soon enough. "Fine, be a spoilsport. Anyway, Tony here, decided to back Santos up. Sort of. He said if Santos had lost, he'd at least have gotten his dick done because he wasn't a pussy like me. Of course, yours truly couldn't pass that up, so I told him we could add onto it—piercing for piercing. I had one nipple done already, so I got the second, and Santos, being the masochistic asshole he is, went straight for his prick. See, I hadn't gone that route since I actually liked to use it on occasion, and letting it heal was a dry spell I wasn't looking forward to, but now I was stuck. When Santos got the fifth one, I was done. I don't even remember if I had to forfeit anything. My dick fucking hurt, and he just got cleaned up and zipped his jeans like it wasn't a problem. But, I do have to say, they are nice to use." He waggled his eyebrows at Eden, who flipped him off.

"As fun as this has been, Marco, I don't want to hear any more about your dick or Santos'. I'm starving. So, what are we eating?"

That was the cue to start arguing over what everybody wanted until we all eventually settled on the same thing. Vanni went to put the order in while Marco and Tony left, the latter promising to fill me in later on issues that had popped up, but that left me alone with Eden.

"Do you want me to leave? she bluntly asked. "I

don't want to be here if it's going to cause problems. I can stay up at the main house with Vinnie until I'm not needed..." She trailed off under the force of my glare.

"Come sit with me. Please." I waited until she warily crossed to the island and took the stool next to me, although she pulled it a couple feet away first. "I don't want you here because it's not safe. That's the *only* reason. And now that you're here, well, we'll just have to deal with it and make sure you stay safe." Blowing out a breath and briefly closing my eyes, I tried to apologize for being an ass. "I didn't mean anything by what I said earlier. It feels like you're leaving me behind, and I've barely digested the fact that my father ruined my life. *Both* our lives. Who knows what else he's done. It's just a lot to deal with, and my knee-jerk reaction was to fall back into blame and jealousy. I'm sorry. I'll try not to pop off with whatever ends up in my head. And," I had to swallow hard before I could finish, praying she didn't take me up on my offer, "if you only want to be with Vanni, or whoever, and not me, I'll understand. We can still be friendly, eventually, I won't lie and say I'm okay with it, but I would do my best to get that way." My stomach hurt at the thought of her friend-zoning me, and my eyes settled on the peony tattoo when I couldn't hold hers any longer.

The black polish she wore registered before the sensation of her tracing a fingertip across the ink that

I'd mostly kept covered for the better part of a decade. It was bare now; I hadn't bothered to put my watch back on yet, and I was considering moving it to my other arm when I decided I needed to wear it again.

"Would you mind if I came to hang out tonight? After dinner, I mean." I couldn't tear my eyes off of the gentle tracing she was doing, but I managed to nod my head. Much to her amusement. "Okay, caveman, words are good too." She sounded lighter, freer than before, almost like she used to, and a stabbing sense of fear suddenly hit me in the chest. Dread consumed me as the fear morphed into a certainty that she would somehow be taken from me.

"Eden, promise me, don't leave this house, under any circumstances, until this is all over with. Do you understand?" I met her gaze then, seeing right through the poker face she was trying to give me. Worry stood stark in her forest green eyes. "Eden?"

"I'll be careful, Santos. But I need to pee, so I'll see you at dinner, and after?" She pulled her hand away as she stood, sadness tinging the smile she tried to force.

I was going to fucking lose her again.

eight
feral love

Eden

I officially had my license again and couldn't wait to show it off. It was a little bonus in the grand scheme of things, but for me, well, it was a big deal for me to be legal and free to be myself. Despite the unrest or the people that followed me on every venture off of the estate, I knew, one day, things would settle down. I'd get to have a life again; whether it would be normal was debatable, but I could deal with it if it weren't. Hell, it would definitely not be, but that was okay. I knew what, and who, I wanted—the rest, it didn't matter so much.

As I headed for my room, the sound of low music playing in the game room lured me, so I detoured, then followed the faint scent of tobacco smoke. It led me to Marco. He stood on the balcony, smoking and staring out over the property, lost in thought.

"Hey, guess what I got today?" I asked, startling

the big guy, but when he turned around, he had his usual crooked grin for me.

"What's up, Paradise? You find Santos' balls in your purse again?" he teased. He just couldn't help giving me shit over Santos and vice versa. The two of us, me and Santos, were well versed in poking at each other, and Marco delighted in pointing out who was currently in the lead and who owed who an apology. I was also pretty sure it was his way of playing peacekeeper, which I'd noticed he did quite a bit. His devil-may-care attitude was totally legit, but so was the more subtle role he'd taken on, and it worked well. "If you give them back again, make sure he keeps 'em this time. The poor sap seriously needs a pair. You've broken our enforcer, Edie," he whined when I laughed. I hadn't, broken anyone that is, but Santos *had* been extra sweet and accommodating, not a trait I was too used to seeing from my ex-boyfriend. I was pretty sure he wanted to be a current one as well, but we still had a bit of old feelings to hash out before I'd chance that it wouldn't blow up in our faces and permanently wreck everything. For now, I was happy with the pace things were going.

"He'll be okay," I reassured, certain I was right. "He's trying to avoid pissing me off. Seems he doesn't like being friend-zoned." I rolled my eyes and pulled out one of my own cigarettes, and as I put my lighter back in my purse, I grabbed my new driver's license and nonchalantly dropped it on the table for Marco to see.

"Well, look at you, all legal and shit! And your picture doesn't even suck." His smile held more warmth, with a hint of pride added in, and I couldn't help but beam back at him.

"I was so nervous I'd tank the test or run over an old lady or her dog or something, but I passed!"

"Of course you did. You're Eden fucking Moretti. You can do any goddamned thing you want to. And if you did run anyone over, or fail, I'd just have Tony get one of the men to make a visit and pay them off. We'd have made sure you got it, one way or another." For a second, I was worried they'd done just that, but the teasing light in his eyes made me *almost* certain that they hadn't. "Have you shown the others yet?"

I shook my head and paused to take a drag from my cigarette as he crushed his out in the ashtray, "I heard the music and came in here to investigate."

"So I'm first today?" he asked with a glint in his gaze that had my heart rate picking up. "I'm going to rub that in Vanni's face, the smug fuck." And then he was crowding me, and I wasn't backing up. His breath, heavy with the scent of tobacco, played across my lips as he kept his eyes on mine. Not that I minded since mine tasted and smelled the same. "You know, that's why I love you."

"What?" I asked, wide-eyed at his declaration.

"That you're first in whatever feud or competition you all have going on?"

"Yes and no. Do you know why I called you Paradise all those years ago? Besides the obvious." I shook my head, having thought it was only a play on my name. "Because you were my idea of paradise. I wanted what you and Santos had, and I wasn't sure I could find it anywhere else. I knew what my life had in store for me. But I couldn't exactly mack on his girl, that would have gone *way* against bro code, so I imagined there was a possibility that if the stars aligned one day, I'd find what I wished for. And now they have, so that's what you are. *My* Paradise."

"What the fuck, dude?" It was his turn to be wide-eyed, and then wariness filled them as he started to step back. I put my cigarette out before I managed to burn one of us, then grabbed him by his belt to tug him back to me. "I show you my license, and you drop all of that on me! I feel like anything I say at this point wouldn't measure up." My shoulders lifted in a shrug, but it wasn't a lie. I was feeling slightly inadequate in the romance department at the moment, yet also kinda tingly with the joy he'd evoked.

"It's easy, Edie. Just open your mouth." He reached for said mouth and pursed my lips like a fish before moving them open and shut. He also didn't get any farther since I *accidentally* pulled my lips free...then bit his finger.

"Ow, you shit, what was that for?" He might have been complaining, but he was laughing too. "Kiss it better." The injured fingertip was thrust back in my face, and I did lean in to kiss it, but I decided to go one better. Before he could pull away, I gripped his wrist and sucked the digit into the warm recesses of my mouth, twirling the tip of my tongue around it for good measure before pulling off with a pop. "That was...unexpected. And really fucking hot. Don't think I'm forgetting where we left off, but Lady Garden's lady garden just got on my mangrove's radar."

My groan of second-hand embarrassment was swallowed up by Marco's lips crashing into mine, and his seemingly favorite new trend of packing me around came into play as he hoisted me up to go inside, barely breaking away to navigate the doorway. A moment later, my back hit the hard, fuzzy surface of the pool table, and I arched a brow at him in question.

"Yep, happening right here, right now, before someone interrupts us. You've been staying with Santos at night, Edie. How am I supposed to party crash the sick room?" His complaint mostly went in one ear and out the other as he pulled his shirt, then mine, off before doing the same with our pants and shoes. We were down to just underwear when he walked off to the bar.

"It's been three days; you'll survive. Why are you

getting a drink?" I'd thought we were doing something else entirely, but maybe he wanted to finish that stripping game we'd played before...

"I stashed these things all over the house while you've been doing things like worrying us to death and getting your affairs in order." He waved two foil packets as he came back to take his place between my spread thighs.

"Little ambitious there, don't you think?"

"Confident, Edie," he replied with a smirk. "It's called confident." And then he shucked his tented boxer-briefs down his thick thighs, revealing his ruddy-tipped erection in all of its pierced glory. "I can't fucking wait to make you scream my name, Eden. The whole fucking house is going to know who you belong to." His promise was delivered with hazel eyes hooded with lust.

"Go on with your bad self then, show 'em how it's done," I teased with a smirk of my own.

"Lose the rest, or I'm liable to damage your pretty underwear. You have until I get this thing on my dick. After that, I can't be held responsible for my actions."

Just to taunt him, and maybe gain a few extra seconds by keeping his attention on me rather than wrapping his prick, I quickly slipped off my lacy panties before I arched up into a backbend, twisting my arms behind me to unhook the clasp of my bra. The maneuver had the desired effect because I swore

I heard something close to a growl come from him, and then he was holding my hips high so I couldn't sink down. Forced to keep the pose, I contemplated complaining that my arms would go to sleep sooner than later, but the wet heat of Marco's mouth covering my core had it coming out as a moan of pleasure instead. *Fuck the arms.* That was about all I could think as he worked me over with his tongue until my legs had gone to jelly, forcing him to hold up most of my weight. As I reached the precipice, Marco gave up the teasing and went in for the kill, lightly latching onto my clit with his teeth while he paired suction and precise flicks of his tongue in a way that had my lungs seizing in my chest. When he ground his chin, just a hint of afternoon stubble, against my entrance, he got what he'd predicted. Me shouting his name as I came on his face.

His cocky chuckle vibrated against me as he laved my sensitive bits with the flat of his tongue until my orgasm settled down, and then he finally lowered me as he rose up, but he didn't release me. Instead, he notched the head of his dick against me and shoved into my slick sheath, not giving me a second to adjust, only stopping when he was buried to the hilt.

"Oh, god," tumbled through my lips in a high-pitched moan. I wasn't sure if it was aftershocks or if the pulsing my pussy walls were doing was signaling another impending orgasm.

Marco slipped one of his arms free, continuing to hold me up with the other, keeping the edge of the pool table from digging into me, while he helped get my own arms out from under my back where they had, in fact, gone to sleep. As soon as I was in a more comfortable position, he hooked the same arm around me, gripping my shoulder to hold me in place —I definitely wasn't going anywhere, not that I wanted to.

"It's Marco, Lady Garden, but I don't mind if you'd rather worship at my altar instead." He punctuated his silliness with a thrust of his hips before he took up a slow rolling motion that had him touching every hot spot inside me, making me forget even my own name.

"Harder, please, Marco," I begged when he kept it up, staring at me and deliberately avoiding brushing against my clit. I panted and arched against him, unable to quite reach the pinnacle I needed to get off again.

"First, say you're mine," he demanded instead of giving in.

I'd have said any damn thing he asked me to at the moment, but I *was* his. Not a fucking lie.

"I'm yours, Marco. Make me come, baby, please," I begged again, and it was enough for him to give me what I needed...his dick pounding into me, his piercings dragging across my sensitive insides while the base of him rubbed against mine.

"And I'm yours, Eden, always." He captured my moans with his lips, nipping at mine before deepening the kiss and sucking hard on my tongue as he pressed deep in my pussy and repeatedly ground his pelvis against my clit. My scream was lost in his mouth just as his groan of completion was muffled by mine.

The sensations didn't quickly subside, and when Marco made to let me go, I wrapped my arms and legs around him and refused to let him move. "Nu-uh, don't move. Just stay still for a minute," I slurred lazily with my eyes closed and sweat cooling on my hairline.

"I'll stay as long as you want. Just don't forget about the condom; I don't want to hear about it if you move around and leave a snail trail on the felt." He winced at the term as if waiting for backlash, but I'd heard worse. "Or get knocked up. One day, when everything is back to normal, I'm going to put a baby Marco in here." He flexed his softening dick inside me, making my breath catch. "But until then, the swimmers stay in the rubber."

I couldn't help but laugh a little, but as I opened my green eyes to his hazel ones, I saw that he was dead serious. And really fucking hot, all flushed and sweaty with his hair mussed. I'd appreciated his cut physique while he stripped down, the silver barbells on his chest only accentuating the picture he made, but I might like this version even better. My torso slid a bit against his with every breath, the sweat making it an easy glide, and the sensation of his piercings rubbing against me made me consider getting a couple more myself. "Maybe one day, we'll have to see how it goes," I said, evading his declaration. He shrugged like he already knew he'd get his way, then changed the subject.

"So, are you going to say it back?" The words he desired were on the tip of my tongue when Santos walked in.

"Oh, come on! Don't any of you know how to use a bed?" He didn't bother to wait for a reply before he stalked back out, muttering about how Tony was going to remove Marco's dick for having sex on the pool table.

I stared after my first love, eyebrows furrowed in worry and a little bit of guilt. I *had* been sleeping with him every night, but other than some sorely needed comfort cuddling on both our parts, there hadn't been much else happening, and not only because he wasn't cleared for full activity yet. Although he must be getting quite a bit better if he'd come upstairs.

"You ever going to put him out of his misery?" Marco asked without moving from his spot.

"Yeah, eventually." I sighed as I snuggled into his chest, still happy in my afterglow despite my concern about Santos' feelings.

"Better do it soon, then. The only person in this

house that might have balls almost as blue as Santos would be Tony," Marco quipped.

I couldn't help but laugh at his ridiculousness, but my interest in Santos, or his dick, had never really been an issue, not after I found out we'd both been fucked over anyway. "He tends to get in his own way. Either he's an ass, or he's walking on eggshells around me." I didn't want to think about it right then since he was starting to ruin my happy, but Marco wasn't quite done.

"Well, Lady Garden, you *are* the woman that got away. The *only* woman. And now he has to share if he wants you back. Cut the poor guy some slack."

He had a point, but I only gave him an unlady-like grunt in return. Too bad I still needed to clean up. A nap right where I was didn't sound half bad, unless Tony came in with pruning shears to defend the pool table's felt, but a bed would probably be better anyhow.

"So, are you gonna say it back or not?" he asked as he leaned down and dug his chin into my chest between my boobs, irritating the skin there with his prickly scruff. It would leave marks, as I was sure it had between my legs if the slight burn was any indi-cation, but I didn't mind. I kinda liked the physical reminders. He kept it up until I winced and wiggled, laughing as I demanded he stop.

"Fine, you mushy, shit, I love you too. Happy now?"

"I'm in fucking paradise, Edie," he shot back with his trademark grin...and a flex of his half-hard dick where it was still buried in me.

I groaned at his horrible pun, but after a condom and location change, I was down for more.

nine
get free

Eden

A week had passed since I let Marco pin me to the pool table, something both Tony and Santos had glared and bitched about, albeit for two very different reasons. I didn't give a crap if they had a problem with it. I thought they just liked to have something not-so-serious to grouch about as they'd been cooped up in the house for weeks under house arrest, their status essentially revoked by Vinnie until shit cooled off.

My forays out into the city hadn't stopped, much to the displeasure of *all* of them, but slowly, I was helping to chip away at their enemies, and when I was home, I was doing my damndest to enjoy myself and cram in every bit of living that I could. A sense that my time would run out any day dogged me and spurred me on in my quest to reconnect with the guys, to make new, lasting memories.

The looks I'd gotten from the men guarding my every move, from a distance, of course, since I was the carrot being dangled about, had been scandalized. I still smiled at the picture they'd made when I told them where I needed to go. For a group of hardened criminals, they seemed to have distinct morals regarding how the women in the upper circles should comport themselves...too bad for them, I was a reformed hooker. I knew my way around just about anything made to fill an orifice or tease an erogenous zone, be it male or female. The shop had had everything I'd needed to implement one of my plans, and it happened to be the one I was currently in the middle of carrying out.

"Fuck, Edie!" Vanni's shout echoed in his bedroom as I buried my tongue in his ass. A muffled "Motherfucker" came through the door from Santos, followed by Tony's laugh. It was closely echoed by my own, which inadvertently drew a moan from Vanni.

"Get it, little brother!" Tony shouted before reminding me of my schedule. "Eden, you have to drive Santos this afternoon. Don't forget."

I didn't bother to answer him, and the pair presumably moved along, or at least I hoped they did. I felt slightly bad for Santos as he had chosen to walk by Vanni's room at a very inopportune time, but I was too busy rocking my mobster's world with a first-class rim job to dwell on it right now. My sensual torture had started almost an hour ago, edging Vanni with a blowie before I moved on to sucking his balls until he was a whining, pleading mess. Now I had progressed to my original target after getting him too worked up to care what I was doing.

"Eden, please, let me fucking cum!" His begging had zero effect on me, and in response to his plea, I pulled back and blew a stream of air on his puckered hole, making it tighten further. "Just get up here and let me return the favor then! You're killing me," he complained after arching up with another groan when I went back to tonguing his hole.

My ministrations continued until he let go of the headboard he'd promised to hang onto and pushed with his thighs to get me to let his legs down from my shoulders. His attempt at a glare was ruined by the light in his brown eyes and his sweat-dampened hair framing his flushed face. He looked too cute to take seriously—and seriously turned on too.

"You ruining my fun, Vanni?" I asked, unable to help but tease him. "Or are you ready for more?"

"Woman, I'm not sure how much *more* I can take before my balls fall off."

"How about I let you put your big dick in me, but I get to try something too?" This was what I'd been waiting for. The challenge was enough to get him to agree. Well, that and the promise of getting off.

"Fuck yes, finally," he crowed before falling back

onto his pillows. "Hop on and ride, Edie. Put me out of my damn misery." He reached for his drawer, pulling a condom out in preparation.

"Sure, but just a second on the rubber. I need you to do something first." He groaned at the hold-up but set it aside and waited patiently, or pretended to anyway.

I turned around and shook my hair back as I slid my feet under his legs, my head turned to watch him, until I was in a version of the reverse cowgirl. Vanni's brow was quirked in question, but I just reached for the corner of the blanket I had hidden my supplies under and pulled a couple out. Both brows rose when he saw what was on his chest.

"And what am I supposed to do with *these*?" he asked, wariness plain in his tone as he stared at the silicone dildo and lube like it was a snake waiting to strike.

"You're going to get me ready to take your over-sized dick in my ass, and you can choose if you want to come in there or use the rubber," I informed him.

"Uh-huh, and what's the catch?" he asked, full of suspicion.

"I'm going to copy you...without the putting-a-giant-dick-in-your-ass part at the end. Sound fair?" His eyes widened when I held up a slightly curved, slimmer dildo. He wouldn't find out exactly what this one did unless he went along with my plan.

"Eden, I'm not sure—" I felt his dick start to

soften against my rear end and worried I'd pushed too far.

I'd sort of figured that would happen if he wasn't on board, but I kept my disappointment to myself while setting aside the toy. "It's okay, Vanni. I don't have to, but I do still want you to. I only have a few good memories with ass play, and they were kinda ruined by everything that happened. I'd like you to give me some good ones if you don't mind." I was putting myself out there, but so had he.

"You let Santos play with your ass?" he asked, shock written all over his face.

My eyes narrowed on him. "Is that a problem? We were experimenting, and I liked it, thank you very much."

"No, it's hot, just didn't expect that. You were a good girl, Edie." At my scowl, he tacked on, "Still are, just a bit more jaded."

"Soo...we doing this? Or you can put the condom on, and we can just have sex, if you even still want to." *How the fuck can it* always *be so damn awkward between us?*

"Have you seen my dick? Fuck yes, I want it in your ass. I nearly have to pay to get—I did not mean to say that," he ended on a wince. I had to laugh, glad I wasn't the only awkward one. "And you can use a finger. Maybe two. We'll see after that." He broke eye contact as he said it, and from the hard swallow, I knew he was nervous.

"You can start first and think about it a bit longer; I can occupy myself," I informed him with a mischievous grin. Lifting up onto my knees, I reached between my legs to grip his dick and pulled it toward me, trapping it between my slick pussy and hand. Teasing him had gotten me going as well, so I wouldn't need the lube just yet.

"How am I supposed to concentrate with you moving like that?" he asked, voice strained as I glided back and forth, using his thick length to rub one out.

"I'm sure you can handle it, Vanni," I retorted, a bit breathless as I kept my movements slow and steady despite wanting to speed up—the glide of his dick against my clit and rings had my empty pussy begging to filled, but I wouldn't do it just yet.

He took me at my word, and a moment later, the snap of the lid could be heard before a cool wetness tentatively touched me between my cheeks. I stopped and reached back to spread myself open, encouraging him to press his finger against my tightly furled entrance. After a few sweeping motions that coated my hole in lube, Vanni found some of the confidence he'd exhibited the night he and Marco had all but destroyed my pussy. The press of his fingertip breached my ass then sank in as far as it could. Figuring he had it from there, I moved my hand in front of me to support me on the bed as I leaned over to give him more access. It had the perk of giving me more leverage to move against him, and soon enough, Vanni had my ass stretched around several digits. I was getting close, and he started meeting me with small thrusts, holding his arm still so I could fuck myself on his hand while I rubbed my pussy up and down his cock.

Sensing he was getting close himself, I sat up enough to shift my weight back on my knees before taking the precaution of using extra lube. Even though I probably didn't need it just yet, I wanted to make matters as effortless as possible. Gripping the base of his dick to keep him from coming prematurely, I carefully probed between his asscheeks with a finger, filling him to the second knuckle while using my thumb to press against his taint. He didn't shy away, thankfully, but his shout of frustration was accompanied by an impatient thrust that forced him to take it deeper. The shout abruptly ended in a whimper, but I couldn't tell if it was good or bad.

"Vanni? Do you want me to stop?" I was carefully pulling back when his free hand slapped my ass, startling me into yanking it out.

"Ahh, shit," he yelped as he flexed his cheeks in response to the movement, but a moment later, he let out a mix between a groan and a laugh. "I swear I've never been this awkward. Just pretend that didn't happen." I didn't acknowledge the embarrassment in his tone, simply humming my agreement while I waited for him to answer me. "The slap was to keep going. I-I liked it," he admitted, voice muffled by what I assumed was his arm over his face.

"Nothing wrong with liking something, Vanni. I was hoping you would. Tell me if you want me to stop or change what I'm doing, and feel free to move up to the toy. I'd rather be well stretched before I take you back there."

It was his turn to hum an agreement, and then our vocalizations were reduced to gasps, moans, and short one-to-two-word directions and demands.

I came with a cry of ecstasy, the dildo buried in me to hilt. I had Vanni's dick in a death grip and two fingers pressed as far as they'd go while I rubbed his prostate, his curses filling the air around us as I refused to let him get off. As soon as the aftershocks faded, I lifted up, letting the object pull from me as I drenched Vanni with lube. That done, I shifted position to notch him at my back entrance.

Both of us were covered in sweat, and Vanni's expression was full of desperation, but I kept my eyes on his as I let my weight do the work. My lips parted in a short whining gasp when the broad head forced my sphincter wide around it, the burn of his entrance resulting in my muscles flexing around him in protest despite the steps we'd taken to make it easier.

My eyes closed in a grimace as the tip popped inside, and I paused as he tensed under me. "I'm fine," I managed in a relatively normal tone, opening my eyes back up to find worry etched on Vanni's face. "It'll feel better once I adjust," I promised, waiting for my ass to accustom itself to the fact that it couldn't tighten back up.

"It feels fucking fantastic on my end, but I know... I don't want to hurt you," he finished, shadows in eyes, and his dick softened just enough to provide relief. I didn't care for the reason; I wanted this to work, but not at his expense.

"Vanni, I'm fine. If I wasn't, I wouldn't do it. If you're not into it, we can clean up, and I won't bring it up again."

He only nodded in return, but the crease between his brows smoothed out. He reached for the lube before adding more to himself, then traced his fingertip around my taut skin where we connected. As he fully hardened again, I reached for the pen-like vibrator I'd stashed out of sight and clicked it on, settling it against my clit while I began to incrementally slide down Vanni's thick pole. When it touched the attached metal, my entire southern region contracted, forcing my slick arousal from my empty pussy to pool on his balls and slip down his crack. The sound that came from me was part guttural moan, part choking gasp. *I'm never going to get used to these things.* Some self-experimentation might be in order before trying anything else with the guys; damn things should have come with an operations manual.

"Edie, if you do that again, I'm going to come," Vanni warned, his hips pulsing up before he forced them back down.

But I wasn't having any of that before I was done. "Squeeze the base of your dick, and don't you dare let go until I say so," I said, delivering a glance over my shoulder that said I meant business. He pouted but did as I said, and I continued to work my way down, only stopping when I came to the ring where his fingers formed the makeshift cockring.

His free hand came up to grasp my hip, fingers digging in to grip me so tightly I'd have fingerprint marks later. Not that I'd mind.

With my ass fully impaled, I upped the speed of the vibrations and started a leisurely paced ride on Vanni's oversized dick, more than ready for the finale. Moans and whimpers escaped me as I rode him harder, matched by groans and near-growls, our bodies straining for completion. And I was about to up the ante because I couldn't hold on much longer.

It was sweaty, messy, dirty, and unapologetic sex between two people that cared to share in their mutual pleasure. Whether I was choking and drooling on myself with his cock down my throat, or making noises more suitable to the barnyard, Vanni was on board. He was my filthy, horse-cock packing, kindred soul when it came to the raunchier end of fucking. The thing was, it *wasn't* just fucking. It was more, and I kinda loved it. I also suspected he wasn't the only one into the filthier side of sex after that night we'd all shared at Cherry Baby. Figured it was only a matter of time before I had more dick than I knew what to do with. I couldn't fucking wait.

"Eden, I can strangle my dick all I want, but it's not going to stop anything, very soon," Vanni panted out from behind him, spurring me on to grab the last toy and coat it well.

"Stay relaxed," was all the warning I gave him as I firmly pressed the thin massager with a curved, egg-shaped head to his asshole and slid it in with one continuous motion.

He arched under me with a shout of what I thought was surprise, and then a "Holy fuck" came out of him when I clicked it on. His hips started slamming into me from underneath, making my tits bounce in earnest, and he abandoned his hold on his dick to grip my hips in both hands, forcing me down to meet him with a sharp clap of skin on each thrust. It was all I could do to keep my balance, but his hold helped steady me while I worked the vibrators for both of us.

A minute later, my shriek was muffled behind my tightly closed lips as I squirted in a gush of fluid all over Vanni and the bed. My muscles clamped down on him, and then his own pulsing orgasm flooded my insides, accompanied by a harsh grunt. He held me tightly to him as he ground into my sore hole, the pain only heightening the pleasure, and before his own pleasure could subside, I pulled the massager from the snug tunnel of his ass.

Discarding everything on the corner of the bed to clean up later, I twisted my legs and leaned back onto Vanni's chest, his half-hard prick still lodged in me, his cum leaking out around it. My back stuck to his chest, both slick with sweat, as was much of the rest of our bodies. I slid my head onto his shoulder and licked my dry ass lips as I looked at him.

"So, how was it?" I asked, slightly out of breath from my exertions.

A hint of a dimple appeared when he smiled, and though the look in his eyes was sated and sleepy, his voice was husky with spent desire.

"I fucking love you, Eden Moretti."

I had to laugh a little, and I definitely needed a cigarette, but... "You better, because I think mounting your dick with my ass says it all." One day, I'd feel more comfortable saying it with carefree repetition, but until then, I was excellent at showing it.

ten
you don't own me

Eden

I checked out my eyes in the bathroom mirror after getting ready, happy that the last bit of red had finally disappeared. It had taken that last corner so long to go away that I'd worried it would be a permanent fixture.

A tap at the open door of my bedroom had me watching the reflection in the mirror until Santos came into view. "You about ready to head out?" At my nod, his eyes dropped, and he shifted uncomfortably. "Are you sure you don't want to stay back? I can get someone else to take me..."

My glare quickly shut him up. "I just finished getting ready. If you don't want me to, that's fine, but I do have my own follow-up scheduled, so I'll be going there anyway."

With a sigh, he met my eyes in the mirror. "It's not that I don't want you to. I just hate that you're a target every time you leave the estate, and with me in the vehicle, it's going to put a bigger target on you. The police aren't above fabricating whatever they want to at this point, but out of sight is out of mind. Putting me front and center with you feels like I'm asking for more trouble."

"That's not an answer, Santos, and I'm a big girl, you know? I can handle making my own decisions, right or wrong. I've been doing it for a very long time. So, are you riding with me, or do we need to see if the furlough approval can be altered? If you don't want to deal with that, you can probably cancel and reschedule." I turned, resting my back against the sink as I crossed my arms over my chest.

"Technically, anyone in the household can drive me as long as they're allowed to leave the property. Hell, I can drive myself, except the doc hasn't cleared me yet." At my glare, he held his hands up, mock fear in his eyes. "I'd love for you to drive me. Thank you for the offer." My lips twitched at his antics, but I wrestled them straight again, waiting for an apology. "I'll meet you in the car and make sure Tony has guards all the way there."

It wasn't quite what I was looking for, but I'd take it. He'd be stuck with me for the next couple of hours anyway, so I could torture him then when he couldn't escape. "We're taking one of the SUVs. They're sturdier than my car and have a darker tint. You're riding in the back."

He glanced back in surprise, then appreciation. "I'm sorry. I should have known you'd take precautions." He took off before I could ask what the fuck else he'd been thinking, but it was just as well. We didn't need to end up in an argument. We were already exceptionally good at unintentionally pushing each other's buttons.

After warnings from Tony on safety and check-ins, a group hug with Marco and Vanni, the two of them cracking enough lewd jokes about me and Santos to make a hooker blush, we were finally on the road.

"You gonna keep staring at me in the mirror like a creeper, or spit out whatever you're thinking?" I teased Santos in the back. He only glanced at me every couple of minutes; the rest of the time, he was uneasily scanning our surroundings. Giving him shit helped the nervousness he was causing me with his own.

"I like looking at you," he finally confessed after a few more glances. "I always did, but now it feels as if I don't have the right, or like I'm going to wake up and find you're just another dream that I can't hold on to."

"You know I won't willingly leave you again,

right? And if you must know, I kinda like it when you look at me too. I always did." My eyes stayed on the road, an excuse to avoid him seeing too much after my admission. I had to protect my heart as much as I could until he made a decision one way or another. He had to accept me as I was now, not try to put me back in the mold of my younger self.

"I think I'm starting to believe that, but it might just concern me more than waking up one day to realize you're gone again. I can't keep you safe! Vinnie has you putting yourself out there, tempting anyone with a hard-on to harm us, and I can't do a fucking thing about it but sit, wait, and watch whatever happens. Besides whatever you have going on with the others, which I don't have an issue with." I did make eye contact then, and my expression was full of the skepticism I felt at his declaration. He blew out a breath and glanced out the window before continuing. "I don't have *many* issues then. If you couldn't be with me, they're not bad alternatives; they'll take care of you just as I would. It's the whole knowing what it was like to have you all to myself while knowing that's not an option now. I've wrapped my head around it, but I just have to get the rest of me on board. Like my possessiveness and jealousy, and maybe a little bit of my heart that's still bruised and resenting that you chose them over me."

My stomach turned at his candid revelations. I hated that he felt that way, but I couldn't fix it for him. The small surviving part of the girl I'd once been and had hidden away for safekeeping wanted to comfort him, but despite the fact that she'd been content and head over heels for Santos, that didn't mean she had never wondered. I couldn't tell him that, likely ever. That had danger signs written all over it, and I worried it would shatter whatever understanding he'd come to regarding our situation.

"You know you could have said that at any time since I've been back, right? And for your information, I did not *choose* them over you. You haven't been excluded, but just as I can't turn my back on you or my feelings for you, the same is true for them."

"I know," he said with a sigh. Frustration was evident in his voice, but unless he fessed up to what else was bugging him, I couldn't help him. "You're the only woman I've ever been with. I've had sex *one fucking time* in my life because every time I tried, all I saw was you. I think maybe that was my subconscious telling me you hadn't left of your own free will, evidence to the contrary, but I was too fucking blinded by hurt and anger to consider it. And you were *gone*. You might have been able to stay off the radar for a short time, but, Eden, there's no way you managed to avoid us for nearly a decade while being right under our noses. Danny had to have known! He liked to keep his insurance close, and he wouldn't have passed up having a trump card with the Carlottis. It's too late to find out what his plans were, if anything, but I suspect he was waiting for Tony to take over. Things just don't add up."

"I've had the same thoughts. Mostly while I was gone. I never really questioned it before because I was happy to avoid you all. Your fath—Rodrigo couldn't have known, or he'd have already..." I decided it was better to end that train of thought. I felt bad enough that I'd reminded him about his shitty parent. We stayed quiet for the most part after that, both of us lost in our own heads, but at least it wasn't as tense as before, his window-watching vigilance notwithstanding.

I was on the off-ramp, going around the sharp curve that would take us to the hospital, when he tried to kill us both.

"I'm fucking horny, Eden. That's my problem," he loudly blurted out, surprising the shit out of me, and I barely held the wheel steady.

"Fuck, Santos, warn a girl. Or, you know, wait until I'm on a straightaway?"

"Sorry," he muttered, waiting for me to stop at the light behind our escort. "I keep screwing it up, and I feel like I'm going to be the guy that's practically a virgin for the rest of my life. Somehow, I manage to come across you every time you're involved with Vanni or Marco, and then I hold you at night while trying to keep my hard-on away from you, so I'm not an asshole. I don't want you to think I only want sex, and we can't seem to find our stride, or mesh, or whatever. It seems like we're stuck in a goddamn limbo of before and after, and I'm tired of it." The enforcer with a reputation others did their best to avoid was actually pouting in the backseat.

"Why are you pussy footing around it, then? You say you missed me, you took over my room when you had your own, and we're cuddling like teenagers, yet you don't make a move. I'm not saying I wouldn't shut you down until the doc says it won't kill you, but you could have at least *tried*. I mean, I'm sorry you couldn't seal the deal elsewhere." I winced, needing to backtrack from my harshness. "Okay, maybe I'm not sorry, because I kind of like the fact that you were still that hung up on me all this time, but you *did* get your dick sucked, so you can't quite call yourself virginal. If you hadn't noticed, sex isn't really a big deal for me. Don't get me wrong, I'm *ecstatic* that I can enjoy it without the rest of the shit that used to come along with it. It's nice to get to experience the other side of things, but sex is sex, Santos. If you're shy, that's fine, but you do deal with your hang-ups regarding the rest of it." Before he could answer me, prolonging this awkward as fuck conversation, I pulled into the parking that had been reserved for us. "We're here. We can talk about this later," I told him, possibly fibbing a bit. He could sort out his own shit. Just like the rest of us had to.

We didn't have to do the regular registration thing; instead, we were escorted to a room where a nurse had Santos' information waiting for him. Perks of being part of the Carlotti heirs' circle, I supposed. Santos ignored the stares from other patients and staff as we passed, but I was happy to stare them down with a hard glare until they stopped gawking at his scars. They weren't *that* bad, not to me, at least. They didn't take away from his good looks. I was glad when we got into a room, so I didn't feel the protective urge to guard him.

"The waiting room is just down the hall if you'd like to head down there," the nurse addressed me, holding the door open. I was about to take her up on the not-so-subtle offer and excuse myself, but Santos had other ideas.

"I'd like my girlfriend to stay." He was polite, but his tone said that anything except agreeing with him wasn't happening.

Shrugging, I took a seat on the chair in the corner of the room while the nurse went about the usual routine of asking questions and taking vital signs. It had been a while since I'd had any type of regular check-ups, but I'd had them done as a child and, in more recent years, at the free clinic when I couldn't kick an illness myself.

I wasn't surprised when Doc came in, although he raised a brow at my presence.

"Are you staying for the duration, then?"

"She is," Santos again answered for me.

Doc nodded as if he'd expected nothing less but wanted to double-check, then turned his attention to the screen of the laptop mounted above the counter before addressing his patient.

"I'm assuming you've discontinued the cane?" At Santos' derisive snort, Doc continued on without comment. Santos had ditched that thing the first chance he'd gotten. "Well, let's get the shirt off and check the wound sites."

As Santos and Doc did their thing, I became the staring creeper. I had to drag my gaze from Santos' tattooed arms and torso since even the scars and weight loss didn't detract from the fact that he was fucking hot. Thankfully, neither of them was paying me any direct attention, and I managed to concentrate on the healing puncture wounds as they were revealed. The skin was pink and somewhat puckered; it would definitely leave more scars, but they looked like they were doing well to me. To Doc, too, it seemed.

"I think you're fine to resume normal activities, pending urine and blood tests," he declared after some poking, mobility tests, and more questions.

The darkly sensual stare Santos directed at me over his shoulder, out of sight of Doc, froze me to my chair. I might have spoken too soon about getting frisky if he got an all-clear. Seemed like I'd have to put up or shut up.

I swallowed, equal parts worried and excited for what that look promised, and pulled my phone out to text Tony the good news to distract myself while Santos finished up.

"Miss Moretti...*Eden*," the doctor corrected, drawing my attention to him. "If you'd follow me to another room, I'll get the nurse to take care of you now and bump your appointment up. I'll move my lunch to later since you're already here."

Santos had tensed at the leaving part, and after hearing his concerns over me being out of his sight while we were away from the house, I decided not to make them worse. Besides, he'd asked me to stay for his, well, demanded, but still.

"I'm fine in here, Doc, nothing this one hasn't seen before," I quipped. Making light of the situation was my usual go-to when I was uncomfortable.

He nodded without argument and excused himself with the promise to be back after the nurse did her thing. Apparently, I wasn't the only one feeling the strain in the silence while we waited on her to appear.

"I don't have to stay if you'd rather have some

privacy. I can take the chair out in the hall, not like anyone can get into the room any other way."

"It's fine," I reiterated with a shrug as I gathered my long black hair up into a bun to get it out of the way.

"It's not if it's making you uncomfortable, Eden. I wanted you to stay for me and my peace of mind. I can get that just fine from the hall." He crossed his arms and stared me down, silently demanding the truth.

"Have it your way, Santos. You're right. I'm not sure I *want* you in here in general, but I also don't particularly care if you stick around. I don't mean that in a bad way, but I'm neutral on the subject. There isn't anything that's going to be discussed or checked out that I wouldn't relay later anyway, so in this instance, it's a moot point." I held my hands up, quirked my lips on one side, and raised my brows.

Our standoff was interrupted by the nurse, and Santos wisely chose to take a seat and shut up while she did her thing. I swore his gaze burned into me like a brand, but I refused to turn and look. Instead, I just sat there, hyper-aware of his attention. I *had* stared at him, though, so I figured fair was fair.

The doctor came in before the nurse finished with my blood pressure, so she quickly marked the results down in my chart and took her leave.

"Okay, so how is everything feeling? Any pain or

other concerns?" he asked as he reviewed the screen with my chart on it.

"Good, for the most part. My ribs hurt if I wear a bra for too long or exert myself too much. Regular pain relievers help, and I don't push it. The bruising is gone, and so is the red crap in my eyes. I even got my license, so my vision must be fine too since they didn't say I needed glasses to drive."

He congratulated me on that last bit, but he didn't crack a smile like I'd been aiming for.

"I'll want a full work-up with a blood draw and urine sample and new scans to make sure everything healed properly." He typed on the laptop, presumably putting the orders in and taking notes, then snapped a pair of gloves on. "If you lie back and pull your shirt up, I'll examine your ribs."

I pulled my hoodie over my head and tossed it to Santos before stretching out on the table and rolling my tank top up to just under my bust while the doc pulled the foot extender thing out so I could lay my legs down. Both me and Doc glanced toward the corner of the room at Santos' noise of surprise.

"Don't mind me, didn't realize you had that," he said, gesturing to the tattoo across my abdomen. I hadn't thought about him not knowing about it yet. Honestly, I was shocked that the others had kept their mouths shut other than vague teasing. Which, come to think of it, was probably not helping the poor guy's irritation.

I shrugged and didn't comment. Doc took my cue and ignored it as he began pushing and poking in seemingly random spots with the same questions, over and over. When he was finally satisfied, and my ribs were on the tender side, he helped me sit up then went to dispose of his gloves and wash his hands.

"Nothing feels off from what I can tell, but you probably need more time to heal. You're still taking the vitamins I prescribed, right?" At my nod, he made more notes and continued. "It could be that you weren't in the best of health before the incident, but the scans will either confirm that you're on the right track, or we'll find something else that needs to be addressed. Moving on—I want to refer you to a specialist for a general visit and an ultrasound of your bladder and reproductive organs. I'm not well versed in that area and would like to cover all the bases before you become sexually active again."

"Geez, Doc, you just want to foist me off to avoid getting charged," I teased at the same time Santos snapped at me.

"Eden!" was all he managed before I stopped him with a glare, not appreciating his sharp tone in the least. Or his intention to be a damn tattletale.

With a groan, Doc ignored my teasing, waiting expectantly for Santos to continue. When he didn't, he turned that look on me.

"I didn't know," I told them both and shrugged.

"No one said I couldn't have sex!"

Doc blinked twice, then took it in stride, much as I imagined he had to do on a regular basis with his line of work and employer. "Refraining wasn't explicitly recommended. I had assumed that you might be hesitant to engage in or would have pain with intercourse."

He shot a glance at Santos as if waiting for another outburst or confirmation that we were doing the deed, then back to me again when the man in question wisely kept his lips zipped.

"Not him." I stuck a thumb out to point at Santos. "He's aiming to get his junk named Gilbert; it has to have passed from blue to purple by now," I joked, earning a smile from the doc, one that he quickly tried to hide when Santos made a noise of disgust. "So far, just Marco and Vanni, but I'll wear Tony down eventually," I kept on. Doc didn't even seem a bit surprised at the fact that I was involved with them all. He knew what was up, had probably known before I had.

"I'm going to strongly suggest that you not use birth control yet, but condoms aren't failsafe. I'd like to get your appointment done with the gynecologist first, then see your body heal more from your malnutrition and injuries before we mess with your hormones. At this stage, a pregnancy might be more detrimental to your health than a contraceptive." He perused something on his screen before moving back to the former topic. "Did you have any pain or bleeding when engaging in intercourse? And how is your cycle? Regular yet?"

I hedged at both questions, wondering if I should have kicked Santos out after all. "Um, my period is still hit or miss, and there hasn't been any blood after sex."

"But there has been pain or discomfort," he pressed, and Santos lost his cool.

"What the fuck, Eden! You didn't say anything. And Vanni is—"

"Shut up, Santos!" I stopped him in his tracks. He didn't need to be spouting off about Vanni's dick. "I kept quiet when it was your turn."

"Mr. DeLuca, I'll have to insist that you step out if you keep interrupting." Doc was nothing if not stern when he wanted to be, and Santos sat back, but I knew we'd be discussing this further later.

"Nothing bad. I would have stopped if need be," I informed the doc while staring Santos down, ready to get the appointment over with. "But the birth control is going to be an issue since condoms can break. Besides, Marco keeps talking about knocking me up, and I'm starting to think he's serious," I mused, only to have Santos get up and stalk to the wall by the door to stare at me dead on. He was well and truly pissed, but at least he was respecting my request for silence to the T. Even Doc raised his brows at that revelation. *Men.* Just when you thought you had them pegged...literally, in Vanni's case. I kept my snicker to myself, highly doubting it would be appreciated. It wasn't like I could explain anyway, not after I'd snapped at Santos for talking about his dick. They *all* might have something to say if I popped off about sticking a vibrator up his ass.

"Miss Mor—Eden," he corrected, getting a glare at the formality and drawing my attention back to the conversation that I wasn't interested in having. "Generally, it wouldn't be my place, but if I need to speak with him..." He left off, waiting for me to say yay or nay.

"He's just fucking with me." I winced at my choice of words, deciding that awkward might just be a new state of being. "Marco made it clear that it's a discussion for later. Can we wrap this up before I say anything else, please?" Thankfully, he took me at my word that it was all copacetic.

"For the time being, I'm going to give you a fairly new type of contraceptive. It's a gel that's applied like spermicide, and it lasts about an hour. It can be used alone, but to be on the safe side, use condoms. And if you have any concerns or need these boys lectured, you just let me know. I'll have the nurse collect you for the tests and get you referred to a colleague." He excused himself after closing the laptop. I got the drift that he wasn't all too pleased with me, but at least he'd stopped pressing to interfere.

eleven
my boyfriend's back

Eden

"**E**den, why didn't you stop Vanni if it hurt?" he demanded as soon as we were alone.

I sighed and held my hand out for the sweatshirt he was still clutching in his hands, putting it on when he handed it over. "It didn't hurt, not like that. Just like I told the doc, I would have put a stop to it. Believe me, I'm perfectly happy to have full control over my sex life. It's *nice* to have a lack of necessity to trade it for basic shit like food and rent."

Santos' bright blue eyes clouded with anger and regret, and he stepped forward, stopping between my spread knees before reaching up to cup my face with one inked-up hand. The slight rasp of his callouses against my cheek made me suspect that he'd been spending time in the gym—against doctor's orders—but I decided to shelve the ass chewing for later. Doc had said he was good to go now anyhow.

He tipped his forehead against mine, making my eyes flutter shut from his close proximity. His breath caressed my lips as he spoke against them. "I'm relying on you to make sure none of us push you into doing anything you don't want to do." At my nod, he lightened up and changed the subject. "What's the tattoo, and why don't I know about it?"

I laughed and leaned back to stare at him, amusement heavy in my voice. "Alright, bossy ass. Or should that be nosy ass?" He smirked, twirling his finger at me to hurry up. I rolled my eyes in response, but I laid back and inched my shirt up before pushing the top of my leggings down to expose the tattoo in its entirety.

One black brow rose skyward as he reached out to trace the edges of the healed playing cards. "I'd say you considered us all yours before you came back, angel." His eyes met mine, full of something I couldn't quite decipher, then they shuttered again as he stared at my abdomen. "I'd complain about being last—though now I know what Vanni has been crowing about for days—but it fits. And I have to ask, did you wear these for me?" His fingertip trailed down to the top of my exposed lacy blue panties that nearly matched his eyes.

"Happy accident," I murmured, wondering if he'd dare to go further. When he glanced up at me, there was as much heat in his stare as there was in mine, and he seemed to come to some sort of decision.

It didn't even occur to me that we were still in a doctor's office where anyone could, and likely *would,* walk in, but Santos, always vigilant, stepped back to pull the curtain from its strap and slide it along its track to block the view of the door. When he came back, he hesitated for a moment, hesitant now that the initial spell had broken. But whatever indecision he'd faced before, he got over it, bending to trace around my navel with the tip of his tongue.

I watched with anticipation as he found the confidence to move his hands from either side of me up to my hips, where he used his thumbs to rub at the sensitive indents beside my hip bones. *He defi-nitely remembers where my spots are.* My body arched into his touch as I let out a breathy sigh of satisfaction and crossed my arms behind my head to give myself a better view. The position pushed my tits out to give the man a clue of where I wanted him next. I didn't even care that it pulled at my ribs now that they'd gotten irritated by all Doc's poking.

"Impatient, angel?" he whispered against my skin, causing goosebumps to pop up all across my stomach. He didn't immediately give in, trailing wet, sucking kisses across my tattoo and over to the crest of one hip before nipping at it with his teeth.

To stifle any noises that might carry, I sucked the

skin on the inside of my lower lip between my teeth, worrying at it to remind myself to keep quiet.

Santos didn't make me wait too long for what I wanted. His inked-up hands, mapped with the raised lines of his veins that I found oddly attractive, slid firmly up my sides, lightening when they reached my ribs, before pushing both of my shirts and bra over my breasts. I hadn't thought that shit through because I couldn't see a damn thing with the fabric bunched up in my face. I was a bit bummed that I couldn't watch anymore, but the thumbs rubbing circles over my nipples had me not caring so much.

"I've missed these," he admitted, replacing a thumb with his mouth.

And then I was glad for the fabric I could smother myself with it as he pinched one stiff tip and nipped at the other. My breasts felt full and heavy the more he tormented them, and the sensations had to be the only reason I missed his other hand slipping under my pants and into my panties. Santos immediately encountered the rings when he reached my slick slit. I didn't give a shit about them at the moment, though; I needed to be filled, like yesterday, and his callous-roughened fingers would do just fine.

"Santos, stop fucking around," I pleaded, lifting my hips to try to get him where I wanted him. But he pinched my clit, not having any of that. Combined with what he was doing to my nipples, it damn near set me off, but it wasn't quite enough to get there. I groaned in frustration when he lifted his head to look at me, one brow quirked up, accompanied by a tweak to my pierced nub.

"This is most definitely new, angel. You have any more surprises in store for me?"

I didn't think he was annoyed, but there was something a bit off with his tone. Like he was frustrated about being left in the dark or out of an inside joke. Figuring it would throw him off-kilter, I smirked and told him what it was. "You inspired me, so now we match. Only I didn't go all out with the rest, just the cross part."

Possessiveness flared in his cornflower-hued gaze as he comprehended my meaning. He didn't waste any time, burying thick fingers into my soaked cunt as he thumbed my clit. His breath was shaky on my lips as his tongue darted out to lick across the seam of mine before sucking the lower one in between his. With a sharp nip from his teeth that he immediately soothed with a repeat from his tongue, he lifted up to stare at my face as he roughly finger-fucked me.

"I'm sort of out of practice. Tell me if I'm doing it wrong," he confessed, a frown on his face.

My back arched, attempting to force him harder against me, and I answered in a breathy sigh, doing my best not to be too loud. "No complaints. Your muscle memory must be aces." I had to bite my own lip as his confidence doubled; he angled those digits higher to press into me just right. Though muffled by my pants, the wet squelching was still audible in the otherwise quiet room.

When a fingertip circled my still vaguely sore asshole, a knock came at the door, followed by the click of the door unlatching. "We're busy," Santos snapped at who I assumed to be the nurse. The door shut again with a muffled apology from the other side, and the adrenaline rush from being an instant away from getting caught had my pussy walls rippling around Santos' hand as I came all over his fingers. He watched me until my head tipped back, and I squeezed my lips together to keep from crying out. When I couldn't take the intensity, and my eyelids slid closed, he took the opportunity to bite at the center of my exposed throat, redoubling his efforts between my legs.

The blunt edges of his teeth transitioned to soft lips that latched on hard and left what I was sure would be a hickey decorated with tooth marks. At that point, my hips weren't capable of holding still, meeting him thrust for thrust, and finally, his finger found its mark without interruption, sliding straight into my backdoor, aided by my abundant arousal. I shoved the sleeve of my hoodie against my lips, unable to contain the scream his wicked fingers induced. A scream I was certain Santos felt through my trachea as he groaned against it while grinding his hips against me, trapping his hand between us until I was practically riding it while he worked my clit with his thumb. The resulting gush of my spent passion coated his fingers and flooded my underwear, but I didn't give a fuck if I had a wet spot down to my knees, not when I was seeing pretty colored spots behind my eyelids.

Eventually, Santos stilled his hand as my own movements settled down, but he continued to rub his hips against the back of it without removing his fingers from me, unable, or unwilling, to stop just yet. He groaned, his lips leaving my throat to bury his head next to my neck, and I wasn't sure if there was enough friction to get him off. I was about to offer my assistance when a firm knock came at the door, followed by Doc's just as firm voice.

"Gilbert! I'm giving you 'til the count of three to get out of my exam room before I come in there!" he threatened, loud enough to alert the whole damn clinic.

That time, the groan was full of heartfelt frustration, but since he sat up, eyes bright and face flushed, I figured Doc meant business, and Santos knew it.

"See what you did? He's going to call me that until I threaten to off him," he grumbled as he pulled his hand from my pants.

I couldn't even answer, too fixated on him sucking my essence off of the fingers that had been in my pussy before going to the sink to wash them. The doc had reached three, but he didn't come in, and I didn't miss the glare Santos threw at the door. Maybe Doc's balls weren't quite that big. Regardless, I sat up and pulled my clothes to rights before kicking off my shoes and shucking my pants to remove my panties. I set them by the sink, planning to wrap them in a paper towel before sticking them in my purse, but Santos scooped them up and deposited them straight into his jeans' pocket like he wasn't kiping my damn underwear. Ignoring my arched stare while I wet the rough, brown paper towels to clean myself up, Santos stood guard to make sure no one walked in on me.

"Just a damn second," he yelled when more rapping came at the door, urging me to hurry, but he didn't move until I'd gotten my pants and shoes back on. The crotch was more than a little damp, but it would have to do. At least they were black, so it wasn't as noticeable as the rager Santos had going on in *his* pants.

"I'll take care of that back home," I promised as I walked the few steps over to him and leaned up on my toes to give him a quick kiss.

"If you don't, I will be," he muttered, albeit with a self-satisfied smile he tried to hide. I imagined he was pretty proud to know that he hadn't lost his mojo in the foreplay department.

I pulled the curtain back, and Santos seized my hand before I could drop it back to my side. We walked out, holding hands like teenagers and giving zero fucks about what we'd been up to, to get the rest of our tests and my new birth control.

My boyfriend was back, and if anyone had anything to say, they'd not care for his reaction, house arrest hanging over his head or not.

twelve

underpass graffiti

Santos

Filled with incredulous fury, I helplessly watched from the backseat of the SUV as Eden deftly avoided the two vehicles attempting to box her in once we took our exit onto a more secluded stretch of road. There hadn't been a cop car in sight after we'd gotten back onto the highway to head home, and at that point, my suspicions had mounted. This shit just sealed the deal on my accuracy...and the fact that it wasn't the first time Eden had done this.

"Where the fuck are our people, Tony?" I snapped out when he answered the phone, ignoring Eden's brief glare in the rearview mirror.

"You're going to have to be more specific, Santos. I don't have a fucking clue what you're barking about," he said, far more calm than he should have been given the situation had he known about it. *Fucking Vinnie, this is his doing.*

"We're on our way home, and these fucks are trying to cause a wreck or some shit. Not one cop has shown up, Tony, and you know they should be up my ass, waiting to cart me back to jail if I step the least bit out of line. There was supposed to be a discreet escort anytime Eden left the estate, and there's fucking *no one here.*" I was beyond pissed, and if it came down to it, I'd be up on actual murder charges because there was no way I was letting anyone touch Eden. Our escort should have made themselves known the instant the first vehicle started to tailgate us, yet that hadn't happened. I knew they had followed us on the way in as I'd occasionally seen them behind us, but the last time I'd caught a glimpse of them was when we'd left the parking lot to head home.

"I'm finding out now. Don't do anything stupid, Santos. We can't afford it," Tony warned. If he said anything else, I didn't hear it since I hung up on him. Fuck him if he thought I wouldn't protect her. I knew he likely hadn't meant it that way, but I wasn't going to back down if shit went south.

"Seatbelt, babe, this might get bumpy," Eden muttered as two more SUVs approached from the opposite direction, one in the wrong lane.

"Angel, do *not* play chicken with them. Just pull over and let me deal with it." Of course she fucking ignored me and kept driving while I went for the gun that should have been under the seat. "Goddamnit, Eden, would you listen for once?!" I yelled, though I was more frustrated that I'd forgotten the firearms had been removed until all this bullshit house arrest mess was over than at her. Not that it seemed to faze her any.

The headlights on both vehicles flashed as a phone rang in the center console, but I was positive she hadn't taken hers out of her purse. One hand stayed on the wheel while the other popped the catch and took out a phone that was most definitely not hers. Not the one Vanni had given her anyway. She put it on speaker and stuck it in a cup holder as a man's voice filled the cabin of our vehicle.

"Get ahead of them and go between us. We'll make room."

Eden's "Got it" preceded the call disconnecting, and she met my stare in the mirror, guilt filling her forest green eyes. "Seatbelt, please."

"You have a lot of explaining to do when we get home, Eden." I didn't need to be the cause of us wrecking, especially when she was pushing the speedometer into triple digits, so I kept my voice even and cold despite my anger. I even put my seatbelt on, taking note that her shoulders relaxed just a bit when the catch clicked shut.

"Just so you know, I gave my word, so you'll have to talk to Vinnie. I wouldn't even say that much if this hadn't happened." She might have felt guilty, but her voice was distinctly unapologetic. I hated it, but she fit right in with the lot of us. She was loyal to what *she* believed in, and somehow, even after everything we'd done, the loyalty was to us. Not to mention the woman didn't know the meaning of 'back down'.

Moments before we were in danger of a head-on collision, Eden maneuvered the vehicle to straddle the dotted line, and the SUVs parted to let her through. I twisted to watch as they closed ranks, slamming on their brakes once she was clear, our pursuers doing the same. My phone buzzed incessantly in my hand, and I absently answered it, keeping my eyes on the shrinking figures exiting the vehicles.

"Santos!" Tony's yell finally caught my attention.

"Yeah, I'm here. And we're good, but Vinnie and I are not. Did you know—"

"I didn't, but we can deal with that later. Are you sure you can get home safely?"

"Yeah, it's being taken care of, unless more show up, but we aren't too far out now." I could hear muffled voices and assumed Tony had his hand over the mouthpiece of his phone, probably answering Vanni and Marco. "Hey, do me a favor and keep the others inside. I need to have a word with Eden when we get there."

My glare bored holes into the back of Eden's seat

as Tony reluctantly agreed and hung up. I thought Eden might try to talk her way out of it, but she remained silent until we finally pulled through the gates and into the garage. We sat in silence, the ticking of the cooling engine the only sound in the space around us.

"You're never doing that again," I growled, unclipping my belt, then hers, before I hauled her through the seats and into the back with me.

"I don't have a choice. I made a promise," she said quietly, clenching her jaw and refusing to look at me.

"You know, I'm really fucking tired of being a bystander, of being unable to protect my loved ones —that circle is small enough to count on one hand. I'm done with this shit, Eden! It stops now."

At first, all I got out of her was a shrug, but then she got comfortable and snuggled into my lap, bringing in a stark sense of nostalgia to temper my anger. The discussion wasn't over by a long shot, but I couldn't pass up the chance to just hold her. We used to sit like this all the time, watching movies or hanging out with the guys. Just like now, she'd tuck her face against my neck, and my hand would automatically come up to rub circles on her back.

"Maybe Marco has the right idea," I muttered, her familiar scent wafting up from her hair. When I didn't finish my thought, she hummed in response, prompting me to spill my guilty desire. "It wouldn't be able to be me or Marco, but if you were carrying Vinnie's grandchild..."

She stiffened before slowly sitting back to stare at me in disbelief. "Did you *not* hear what Doc said about that? And what the actual fuck, Santos! You're just gonna have Tony or Vanni knock me up, so I'm grounded to the estate?!"

It was my turn to shrug. I wasn't about to apologize for considering any and all avenues to keep her safe, but... "I didn't say I would, but you can't blame me for thinking about it, angel. I'd do anything to keep you out of the situation. It was one thing to get your license and a check-up, but I know you've left for more than that. I don't care for the implications that that little stunt back there has made."

Brows arched, she gave me *that* look, the one that said I was an idiot. "Um, have you not considered that I'd like you safe as well? That your safety might be the only reason I offered to come back early?"

A groan tore from my chest as I thumped my head back against the seat. She was right, but I didn't have to like it, and I'd be plotting with Tony to put an end to her escapades.

"I can see that we aren't going to agree, so maybe we should shelve this discussion for later and head on inside. The others are probably waiting to hear how everything went." It was a flimsy excuse since we'd both texted them with live updates, but I was two seconds from reverting to caveman tendencies like clubbing her over the head to lock her up or staking my claim with my dick to prove she was mine. Maybe both.

As if she read my mind, she brought up my heat-of-the-moment promise from earlier. "You still planning to take care of yourself if I don't?"

"I'm fairly positive that your near-death experience took care of that problem," I retorted, amusement lacing my tone.

"I thought you lived for danger, that it got you all hot and bothered and shit?"

"Yeah, when it's not *you* who's the one in danger. I thought we just went over that." When she just stared at me, the lightbulb went off. There I was, trying to be all gentlemanly and keeping my dick in check while she had other ideas. "I take it that it got *you* all revved up? Or are you after my virtue?"

"Well, I already took that once, but I wouldn't mind a repeat. We never did get to do the teenage sex in a backseat rite of passage." I was positive she'd done plenty in the backseats of cars, not that I resented her for it, but I kept my mouth shut, also not interested in getting shanked a second time.

"When you put it that way..." I didn't waste any time or give her any to change her mind. Dick staking claim apparently *was* an option.

Tipping her back onto the bench seat, I slid to my knees on the floorboard, glad there was enough room to maneuver. Her squeak of surprise when I yanked her pants down was cut off as I folded her legs back to get at her bare pussy. From the abundant moisture coating her flesh, my hypothesis was correct; I wasn't the only one who got turned on by the adrenaline rush of escaping sketchy situations.

I gripped her thighs in my hands, holding her steady as I cleaned up every bit of her offering with my tongue, planning to get her off again before I sank into her tight, wet heat; there was no way I'd last long once I was inside her. But the shoes sailing past me, and then her pants, had me looking up through her spread thighs. And fuck, if the sight of her ankles nearly on either side of her head didn't have my dick ready to stage a mutiny to escape the confines of my pants...

"Get your ass up here, DeLuca, and hand me that paper bag," she demanded, excitement brightening her green eyes.

I hesitated, worried about hurting her. I wasn't as big as Vanni, but I wasn't far off. "Are you sure, angel? I'm not interested in causing you any more pain than I already have."

Her gaze softened before she reassured me. "I know you aren't, and it didn't—doesn't hurt like that. Promise. Now grab that bag so we can figure out how this shit works."

I arched my brow at the 'we' part but did as she asked. She opened the foil, zippered baggie, and pulled a filled tube-like syringe out. I didn't have long to wait while she read the instructions and then handed the thing to me.

"Slide the applicator in, and when you get to that part, stop and push the plunger."

Blinking. That's all I could manage, staring at her hand like she had a live grenade.

"Santos! Don't be a pussy, babe," she goaded me, snapping me out of my trance.

"You know, if this is revenge for me talking about knocking you up—" I shut up, backtracking like a motherfucker once she started to close her legs. "Teasing, angel, just teasing. I don't mind doing it. Really," I said in earnest as she stared, not appearing to believe me. I took the thing to prove my point, then settled one of her legs on my shoulder. She got my drift and propped the other over the back of the seat, spreading herself wide for me.

"I can do it. I didn't think you'd care," she ventured, holding her hand out.

"I love you, angel. I already said I'd do anything to protect you, and that's what this stuff is supposed to do. Least I can do is put it where it goes." I eyed it before I brought it up to her entrance, one last question on my tongue. "Uh, this stuff is safe, right?"

"The warning says it can burn a bit and to discontinue if the discomfort is too bad or either partner develops a rash or something like that." She laughed as she took in my horrified expression.

"What the fuck, Eden? Is it battery acid?"

"Relax, I'm sure it's fine. If not, it washes out." She shrugged, completely unconcerned.

I was so not fucking certain I wanted that shit near my dick, but surely Doc wouldn't intentionally give her anything bad...I hoped.

"Yeah, so, uh, here it goes." *Fucking lame, you idiot, what else would you do with it?* Setting my concerns aside, I slipped the thing into her and watched for any flinches or complaints when I pressed the plunger to empty it. When nothing bad happened, she twirled her finger for me to proceed, and it took a second to figure out what she wanted. Cue dumbass moment number two—I was supposed to take it back out.

"Next time, I'll handle it. That was kinda awkward. And we have an hour, so..." Eden crooked her finger, presumably wanting me to climb aboard, but my dick had decided it was outie, not to mention I was still holding the fucking applicator. It was a bit too late to ask if it was safe to get in my mouth, so *that* was out. "Santos? Just put it in the bag. I'll get rid of it later, but I'm kinda starting to feel like I'm at a gyno appointment, so unless you're playing doctor, which I wouldn't be against, then we should probably get to it before it wears off."

I discarded the empty tube and tried to figure out how to tell her that I wasn't really in the mood anymore without hurting her feelings. My phone buzzed, forestalling that thought, and while she gave me a 'what the fuck' glare when I pulled it out, I couldn't dismiss a message that might be important. Only a few people had my number or any reason to contact me. As soon as I read the message, I changed my mind. Tony had said he'd gladly take my place if I couldn't handle it. The kinky bastard was watching us, but I wasn't about to allow him to take my place. Fuck that noise.

"Hey, it's okay if you don't want to. I suppose it was a bit of a mood killer." She tried to hide her disappointment, and while that didn't do my soft prick any favors, I wasn't about to let her feel bad for what should be a joint effort anyhow.

"No, just want you facing the windshield. We have a peeping-Tony for an audience," I informed her. "Let's give him a show, baby."

She grinned, totally on board with my plan, and the thought of being watched while I made Eden come on my cock had me half-hard, cementing my previous suspicions that I had an exhibitionist streak. I stripped while she positioned her shoulders between the front seats, hands resting on the center console. The center seat worked just fine to position me behind her, and I gripped her hips to guide her back until her legs were between mine, enabling her to sink down on my full-fledged erection. It was going to be a tighter fit this way, but she'd be able to control the depth and speed. At least for as long as I could hold still.

"You're really going along with the 'me taking care of it' part, aren't you?" she tossed over her shoulder as the bare head of my cock settled against her entrance.

"Of course, now ride me, angel. We're on a time limit."

She followed my command, working her tight sheath up and down over my engorged length until she'd gotten all the way to the base. Each time she encountered a barbell, her breath caught in her throat as she flexed around me, and the resulting sensations on my end hit me right in the balls. There was no way I was going to last, and that point was pressed home when she started bouncing back on me. The cross must have been doing it for her because she ground down until she sat in my lap with her hands gripping my thighs. Unable to take it, I pushed her back into position.

"Eden, baby, I'm going to come if you keep doing that," I warned when she complained.

"Not too worried about it, Santos. It won't take me long to finish myself off if it happens." But she kept her hands on the console and went rigid as I took over, yanking her back to meet me as I thrust into her drenched cunt, stretching her out on my dick and making her clench as I bottomed out.

I couldn't get at her clit with my fingers, but there were other things I *could* do. Widening my legs to make room for my hand, I worked in two fingers alongside my cock, her breathy sigh accompanying the move when I put more pressure on her already stressed opening. I used them to angle her pelvis up, encouraging her to work herself on me again. At the first drag of my dick against her sweet spot, she sped up, using a grinding-rolling motion of her hips to keep me hitting where she needed it. I couldn't hold on any longer; my dick throbbed inside as my cum pumped out, filling her up amid my groan of relief. But I would make damn sure she got off before we got out of the vehicle.

"Santos, fuck!" Her head tipped back as I slid my thumb into her ass, pressing against the thin membrane to meet my fingers from the other side. Each push and pull had the dual effect of massaging that piece of flesh, and Eden lost her rhythm to press down hard against me, using short jerks of her hips to prolong the climax. A sharp, short wail preceded her pussy soaking my dick and balls as liquid was forced out, and I imagined her eyes were clenched shut and her lips parted in her throes of pleasure.

Tony better have taken still shots to share with me, or I was going to kick his ass. It was about the only thought in my head as I pulled my fingers free from Eden and removed my shirt to wipe them off. "Come here, angel," I requested, leaning forward to slip my arms around my limp girlfriend and guide her back to rest against my chest.

Neither of us bothered to interrupt the silence,

comfortable and in sync at last. I didn't even care that our commingled mess was leaking all over the leather seat as my prick softened inside her. I was just happy to be able to hold her again, to connect again. And not just the sex, although that was a definite perk.

"Think Tony is going to be pissed about the cum all over his car?" she asked, her head tipped back on my shoulder. I laughed, jostling us both, and my dick slipped out with another trail of ejaculate, making Eden groan. "Yeah, I'm going with a yes. It's not fucking funny either. He had a hissy over the pool table...maybe I should go get some stuff to clean it up. I'm sure there are cleaning supplies in one of these cabinets."

"Eden, baby, breathe. Tony isn't going to care, and even if he did, I'd kick his ass if he was a dick to you. Besides, this one is technically mine." I shrugged when she turned to give me a look full of disbelief. "I have money, angel, quite a bit of it. Tony doesn't pay for everything."

Chagrin overtook her expression as an apology tumbled from her lips. "I didn't mean it like that. I just assumed it was his house, and you have your car... I don't think you're a bum, Santos. Criminal, sure, but not a bum."

"I'm not offended, angel," I reassured her, then dipped my head, unable to resist kissing her pouty lips.

Of course, her phone had to chime right then, but at least it was the one in her purse, not Vinnie expecting more out of her today. As she pulled it out, I peeked over her shoulder, not feeling a bit guilty about reading the message. The sender said Mob Boss In Training, and then the attachment opened, revealing an angry, purple-headed dick squeezed tightly in a familiar fist, with streaks of cum covering a man's chest and stomach. The caption read, *See what you do to me?*

I blinked, somewhat shocked by my best friend. "Did Antonio Carlotti just send you a fucking dick pic? After he jacked off while watching us?"

Eden's carefree laugh warmed me as I reached for my underwear. The garage had climate control, but it had gotten chilly enough now that the sweat had cooled on our skin that we needed to get inside.

"Well, I guess you can pass the Gilbert torch on now," she teased as she commandeered my shirt to clean up between her legs before getting her pants back on.

"Fucking A, baby. Fucking. A." She had my full agreement on that front, and I couldn't wait to get inside to let Tony know. Eyeing the drying mess on my upholstery, I figured the shirt was a total loss, or maybe a souvenir, and used it to swipe at the seat while Eden climbed out through the front, leaving me and my shit-eating grin to follow.

thirteen

fool

Eden

My tits were gonna freeze off if the fuckers didn't take the bait soon. As the days got shorter, the nights got colder, and standing on a corner in fishnets, a skirt that let the edge of my un-pantied ass hang out, and a tube top, sans bra, was *not* something I enjoyed. I also had to admit that in hindsight, not having to troll the streets for johns after Danny recruited me to work at Cherry Baby had been a blessing. A shitty one, but a blessing nonetheless.

With Danny gone, I'd wondered what would happen to the club and the girls, but it appeared someone had already taken it over. They hadn't even bothered to change the name. As I rode by on my way here, I got my first new glimpse of the club, and there had been a line at the door with the usual bass beat carrying out into the night anytime the door opened. Thankfully, I didn't feel much in regards to the building, not that I was eager to see it or anything.

It wasn't like I was going back there, ever, but I also hadn't planned on being hooker bait either, yet there I was, having just turned down the third dude of the night because he wasn't who I was trying to attract. I was about to call it quits when the signal came from across the street. My mark was near. Nerves swarmed my belly until I thought I was going to puke.

Vinnie had assured me they'd try to take me instead of just taking me out, but right then, he wasn't the one with his life on the line and his ass, literally, out in the wind. The dark sedan slowed as I sashayed to the edge of the curb and propped my foot on the fire hydrant, showing my goods to anyone who bothered to look. When it came to a stop next to me, the window lowered, and a decent-enough-looking guy grinned at me.

"Hop in, baby. Daddy needs some ass," he directed as the door locks audibly disengaged, and he flashed a wad of cash at me with a fifty on the outside. But my instructions were to get him alone, not get in his car.

"Sorry, I don't do cars, but I can meet you right back there." I pointed toward the darker alley, a single street lamp lighting up the entrance. Dude looked like he was about to argue, so I shrugged and waved him off. "On second thought, I think I'm going to call it a night. If you head about half a block down, there are several ladies who would be more than happy to assist you." I let my foot slip off the hydrant, smoothed my skirt down, and started to walk off in the direction I'd mentioned.

"Get your ass in the car, whore," he growled at me. And, of course, the fucking signal came again. *Goddamnit.*

"No. Follow me or don't, but your dick won't suck itself." I changed my trajectory and picked up my pace, glad there wasn't ice to make the pavement slick. I barely kept myself from jogging in the stiletto boots, not wanting to draw undue attention to myself, but I was intent on making it back there before he did—hopefully to the safety of the Carlotti men that were supposed to be backing me up.

The man cursed then rolled the window up, speeding off down the street, making a U-turn at the intersection right as I rounded the corner of the building and disappeared into the shadows of the alley. I didn't dare ask if anyone was waiting for me; I was too worried I might be overheard and give the men away.

My palms prickled with sweat, and I took a moment to rub my flower-shaped birthmark with my thumb for luck before finding a clean-ish spot on the cold brick wall to prop myself against. With one foot planted, knee up, and knife easily accessible in case shit went down, I was as ready as I was going to get. I didn't have more than a cursory idea of how to use it, but jab and stab seemed fairly straightforward.

The alley wasn't wide enough for two vehicles, but there was plenty of room for one. The car crept in, stopping just shy of my position, blinding me with the headlights only to shut them off and leave me seeing spots. By the time my vision cleared enough to make out shapes, the man had his door open, bitching at me to hurry up and suck his dick. With the amber running lights still on, I could see him moving—probably opening his pants. He really wasn't going to get out of his car.

Wistfully, I glanced at the tip of the hilt, just barely visible in the top of my knee-high stiletto boots. I couldn't stall any longer, and no one was coming to my rescue. *Surely, Vinnie doesn't mean for me to actually service anyone.* Dread settled in my gut when it started to look like I might actually have to touch the man. *I can't do this.* But I could...I had before, and if I had to now, then so be it.

Kicking off the wall, I pushed my reluctance down and channeled Angel. Not Santos' angel, but Angel the stripper. Angel the whore. That Angel, she didn't mind putting a sway into her step or letting her hips swing suggestively as it made the micro-skirt inch up for her pussy to play peek-a-boo out from under it.

"'Bout fucking time you got your sweet ass over

here," he said as I rounded the open driver's side door to find he did indeed have his half-hard dick out, waiting for me. "Get on your knees. I tried to be nice and let you get in, so don't go bitching about the pavement being cold or uncomfortable."

As I sank down to take my position, I tried to spy anyone coming out from the shadows. *Where the fuck are they? Vinnie is going to have some fucking explaining to do.* And so was I. The guys were never going to forgive me for this. The memory of Tony's arms crossed, fury twisting his face up into a mask of anger, flashed through my head as I came closer and closer to crossing a line I had never intended to even approach again. He'd been so pissed when I left. Even if the others took me back after this, I doubted he would.

"You thought you were so fucking smart, didn't you, *Angel*?" I didn't have a chance to run. My lurch backward was brought to an abrupt halt by two hands grabbing my hair to pull my head up, making my scalp scream in pain while my neck strained at the harsh angle he forced upon it.

"I didn't think anything. Let me the fuck *go!*" I tried to pull away, hair be damned. He could keep the shit, but I couldn't get any leverage to do so.

"Don't play dumb, you fucking cunt. You've been traipsing around town with your bodyguards in tow, but word is out. You got kicked to the curb today. Imagine my surprise when I got tipped off that you were already looking for work tonight. Boss wants a word with you, but first, I'm getting a little extra for my effort."

What the fuck is he talking about? Did Vinnie set me up? With the lack of rescuing going on, it was a distinct possibility, and if so, I really *was* screwed. And who knew what the guys would do, or if they even knew or cared...

I flicked my gaze around in vain. There still wasn't another person in sight. If I screamed, someone might come, but whether it would do me any good was another matter entirely. This wasn't the part of town that kindhearted people frequented after dark. Hell, they barely came around during the day.

The man let go with one hand, giving me a brief spurt of hope that I could get away, but the gun he pulled out buried that real quickly. With his arm draped over the steering wheel, he used the hand in my hair to pull me forward.

"Bite me, and I'll put a hole in you. Boss didn't say you had to be in one piece."

"I can't reach." And I couldn't. My struggles had only served to pull my knees nearly under the car, and while the heat it put off was welcome, the bits of gravel and whatever other debris digging into my skin was not.

"Then sit up, but don't try anything. Hands where I can see them. Just so you know, stall tactics won't work. The boss isn't stupid enough to think the Carlotti boys would actually let you go. The minute you acknowledged the pricks watching you, trying to trap one of us, they were dead. No one is coming to help you, girly, so get with the program."

God, he was a mouthy fuck. I preferred the ones that just got it over with. Hoping to speed things up, and maybe get a chance when he inevitably made me get in the car, I put my hands on his thighs and scooted my legs back, wincing as I felt the skin across my knees break. *Never could keep a pair of fishnets in one piece.* I nearly let out a hysterical bubble of mirth at the thought, but before it could leave my lips, it turned into a whimper of pain when the man wrenched my head forward with his makeshift handle.

Steeling myself for what I was about to do, I closed my eyes, wet my lips, and took the spongy tip of a stranger's dick in my mouth, just like old times. Too bad I had to be sober for it. Soon enough, he was pressing me down to take the slightly above-average cock into my throat. I balked, afraid he was going to come in my mouth. I really didn't want him doing that without a condom.

"Shut up," he snarled at my noises of protest, abandoning his weapon on the dash to take my head in both hands before tipping it up enough to make eye contact. My lips were still stretched around his erection as he let me know exactly why Vinnie had targeted him. "Your boyfriend struggled too when I popped his cherry. Squealed like a little bitch as I ripped his ass up," he bragged, not that I could see Vanni, or any of them, making such a sound. "Too bad you're used up, I've developed a hankering for tight holes, and after seeing the footage of you taking the Carlottis together, there's no way you have a cherry anything."

He raped Vanni. Motherfucker was dead. I bit down, not caring that it would likely get me shot, or worse. Luckily, the idiot must have forgotten about his gun in the throes of his pain and panic as he tried to pull me off, bellowing like a wounded animal. *Who's the bitch now, asshole?* I didn't have any direction in mind when I pulled the knife from my boot. My only intention was to separate his violating dick from its host, but as I let him go, his yanking pulled me off course, plunging the knife into the fold of his thigh. I pulled it right back out, amid his screams of agony, and fell back as his hands released me to cup his crotch. Scuttling back in an awkward crabwalk, I came up against the brick of the building behind me and tried to get to my feet.

With pure, unadulterated hatred in his eyes, he reached for his gun. But his movement let off whatever pressure had kept his more severe wound closed, and a spurt of blood arced up, hitting the window of the open door before ricocheting off to spray across the ground. Several more followed, and he abandoned his firearm to clamp a hand against the wound, but it didn't do him any good. A moment later, his head lolled back as he lost consciousness.

I managed to gain my feet and promptly threw up, splattering them in vomit. I'd never killed anyone before. The sensation of my knife sliding into him, that small pop as the tip burrowed through his skin, to the sucking pull when I'd jerked it back out replayed over and over in my head until I was dizzy with it and my stomach was down to dry heaves.

My feet stumbled away from the scene, yet I didn't let go of my bloody weapon. I had to get back to the estate, but I needed to find a phone first. Mine had been left in the car that dropped me off.

My startled scream echoed around me even as my arm swung the weapon at a figure coming around the corner. The man just barely caught it before I could bury the deadly metal into his stomach. Then recognition hit.

"Fields?"

fourteen
bad dream
Eden

"**J**esus, fuck, Eden! Point that thing somewhere else," Fields whisper-shouted at me, keeping hold of my arm until I pulled away. As soon as he saw the blood coating the blade, he peered around me, then started urgently questioning me. "Whose is that? Are you alone? Fuck, are you *okay*?!" He tried to reach for me, using the flashlight on his phone to see better, but I wasn't quite ready to be touched. I quickly stepped back, wobbling when my heel caught a pit in the asphalt before catching my balance.

I could only stare as I tried to think of what to say. Even if I didn't go to jail, there would be repercussions. Although that was already likely if Vinnie's men really *were* dead. "Are you going to arrest me?" was what I finally blurted out, causing Fields' brows to raise.

"Is there a reason I should?" he countered, then walked around me toward the still idling car, pulling his gun out as he went. "Who's in the fucking car, Eden?" he snapped before shining his light inside.

"I-I don't know. He didn't tell me his name."

"Was he forcing you? Are you hurt? Answer me, damnit, before anyone else shows up!" He kept his voice down, but the way he was scanning back and forth, from one end of the alley to the other, led me to believe that he knew more than he was letting on.

"How did you find me?" My suspicion was blatant, and while he tore fabric from the man's clothes and started wiping down the handles, I edged closer to the exit.

"I didn't. I just got lucky. Please tell me if you're hurt and anything you touched," he pleaded as he shined his light onto the pavement. He let out a curse at whatever he saw. "Is this blood yours? Hey, wait, don't take off! Seriously, Eden, I'm not fucking around."

His warning didn't mean shit to me. He'd been an ally in the past, but this was too coincidental. Not caring that my knees and scalp burned, or that I still held a murder weapon, albeit tucked close to my side, I raced down the sidewalk, hoping to find somewhere to hide until I could regroup. The street was thankfully empty because most people were in the bars or clubs if they were down here this late, so I only had to dodge around the occasional legs of a hobo or the drunks staggering to their next destination. The clack of my boots hitting the pavement was too loud in my ears, a dead giveaway to anyone following, but I was more worried about breaking one of the heels, and subsequently, my neck if I fell.

I made it two blocks before the shine of headlights made me dash between two buildings and cram myself behind a dumpster. With my hand over my mouth, I tried to calm my breathing, but it only picked up when I heard the rapid slap of footsteps go on past me. It was only a minute later that I heard a low "Fuck!" and watched Fields bend over to catch his breath with his hands on his knees. I couldn't move, not without making noise, and I couldn't do anything to shield myself from his field of vision when he inevitably turned around. There was no way I could outrun him. I might be in decent shape, but he didn't have to avoid running into anyone else, which severely limited my ability to escape him.

The glow of headlights filtered in from the street, but they were taking forever to pass, and when Fields swore again, I realized they were going slow, *too* slow. I also realized I wasn't the only one wanting to stay out of sight when the detective hauled ass back my way and slipped in beside me with a glare.

"You know, if you'd have just fucking helped while I cleaned up, then come with me, we wouldn't be hiding behind a goddamn dumpster." He was irate, but his furious whisper lent credence to his complaint. *We're being hunted.* Or at least I was. There was no other likely explanation. Before I could form a reply, the car sped up and flew past our hiding place; it looked much like the one the dead man had driven. "We need to go. They probably found Frank's body. When they don't find you, they're going to bring in more men. Your little stunt tonight has Rodrigo determined to get his hands on you."

"I'm not going anywhere until you tell me how you found me." It wasn't a complete bluff; I *was* running the first chance I got, but not necessarily with *him*.

"I've been keeping an ear out since I got suspended, so I heard chatter that you were on the street and started cruising. This place is usually flush with hookers, yet they were cleared out tonight. Their pimps probably got word, and...it was an educated guess. I'm a fucking detective; finding people is part of my job. Or was. Can you just come with me? I'll get you back to your precious mobsters. And you'd better keep your ass behind those gates until this shit is over." Then he started muttering under his breath. "I cannot believe they actually had you come back, let alone dangled you as bait for that piece of shit."

The need to defend the guys was immediate since they had been so very against my involvement at all. "Wasn't their idea or their fault. They can't move, and, well, I don't one hundred percent trust your ass right now, so that's all I have to say on the matter. Get me out of here and back to the estate, and I won't shove this somewhere vital." I flashed my bloody knife in warning, making his eyes widen.

"Are you insane? Get rid of that! Who the fuck packs around a murder weapon?!"

"I'll ditch it later. Right now, it's the only thing I have—" I stared at him aghast as he disarmed me before I could blink, even with the tight quarters. He stood and opened the lid to the dumpster, the pungent aroma of rotting trash not so bad in the cold night air, and fished out a ratty piece of what appeared to be an old shirt. After he wiped the knife down with it, he threw both items in and eased the lid down, so it didn't bang shut.

"That'll have to do for now. I'll give you a new one once we get to my car." He eyed my stiletto boots with disdain. "Not sure you're going to make it in those, but bare feet would be worse." He edged out from our hiding place, keeping close to the wall as he made his way toward the street. "Get ready to run."

It was an anxiety-ridden, panic-inducing game of hide and seek all the way to Fields' car. My body was covered in both the sweat I'd worked up, racing from shadow to shadow under the detective's careful direction and the cold sweat only shot nerves could produce. And I really needed to fucking piss, but I hadn't had a good opportunity to pop a squat, and there was a distinct lack of clean material to wipe with. Hopefully, the trip back was quick because I doubted it was safe enough for a pit stop.

"Don't slam your door," came from Fields as the locks disengaged, momentarily distracting me from my over-full bladder problem.

"No shit," I snarked back, getting in and closing the door softly. Of course, the fucking thing didn't latch all the way, so I had to yank at the handle until it settled into place. As dire as the situation was, Fields' muffled laughter was contagious, and I had a hard time fighting a grin. I was sure I looked ridiculous, trying to get it shut with my tits about to escape my top, but... "Shut up, asshole. You could have gone around and bumped it for me." My rebuke had a distinct lack of heat, yet he sobered all the same.

"Keep your head down. I'm going to try my damndest to get us out of here." With that grim proclamation, he started the car and eased out onto the road while I slouched down in my seat until I could barely see out the front and side windows.

We made it past Cherry Baby, neon lights washing the interior of the car with their usual red hue as if it were a portent of what was to come, without a hiccup, and beelined through the backroads to get into Carlotti territory. Both of us lost a bit of our tension, but we weren't out of the woods yet. We wouldn't be until we were much, much closer to the estate. As we hit the highway, I thought we'd made it, that my silent bargaining to never do something so stupid and brazen again had worked. Until the bubblegum lights lit up behind us.

"What the fuck, Fields. Were you speeding?" I demanded, my high-pitched voice revealing my fear.

"Don't be an idiot, Eden. You know I wasn't. Lean over here, make it look like you're giving me head." He didn't even look at me, his eyes trained on his rearview mirror as he slowed the vehicle before pulling over.

Knowing I had no way to explain my torn-up stockings, destroyed makeup, and ratty hair, not to mention I probably had blood on me somewhere, I kept my head low and leaned over the emergency brake. With shaking hands, I got his pants open, then partially down, when he lifted to help me, but when his soft dick came out, he grabbed one of my wrists.

"Do not touch my dick! Better yet, try not to breathe on it." As if realizing how harsh and judgmental he'd sounded, he apologized. "I didn't mean... I'm sorry, just, I can't do that."

"It's okay," I said, drawing my own conclusions due to his lack of erection. "I'll keep away as best I can. You could have just told me you don't swing that way. Although, if it comes down to sucking you off to get out of this, you're going to have to take one for the team."

"Pray that it doesn't come to that," was all he muttered before putting the car in park and rolling the window down. The crunch of footsteps on the loose gravel heralded the officer's approach, but a bobbing light played through my window as well. Loudly, while fisting my hair, Fields snapped at me, "Did I fucking tell you to quit?!"

I made slight head motions, hoping it would be good enough since I was trying to avoid getting too close to the now marginally interested appendage.

"Evening, officer," he popped off like getting head while being detained was an everyday occurrence for the police, though around here, maybe it was.

"Fields," the deep-voiced officer greeted as a light came directly through my window, followed by a muffled whistle.

"Think someone forgot their undergarments, Clay," the other officer yelled. There was little I could do to cover up, but someone seeing my lady bits wasn't really a problem I was too worried about. Half the men in the city had probably seen my twat at one time or another.

"I believe you have who we're looking for, detective. Wait, that's right; you're still suspended until you can prove your loyalty," the man drawled with false disappointment. "So, you want to explain why you haven't called this one in?" I assumed he meant me, and I couldn't help but tense at the implication that he was *not* on my side.

"Why do you think I have her sucking my dick,

you moron? You know, this is why you'll never make it past a beat cop. You don't have the brains to realize that if she can't see where she's going, she can't kick up a fuss about it. *And* I was getting a blow job out of it. Thanks for ruining that, by the way." He released my hair and pushed me back before slipping his underwear and pants up, ignoring my accusing stare the entire time.

"Fuck you, Fields. Roscoe, let the boss know we have her and will be there soon." The cop was pissed, but he didn't have anything on my level of fury. I was going to fucking gut Fields the first chance I got.

"Sorry, boys, she's *my* catch. You're welcome to follow and collect whatever praise you'd like for being second place." Ignoring the cursing and refusing to unlock the door when Roscoe tried the handle on my side, he started the car and slipped it into gear. "Better get in your car, Clay. You can't escort me in if you're standing on the side of the road holding your dick." As he rolled up his window and accelerated, he tried to apologize, but I wasn't interested.

"You two-faced piece of shit, I knew I shouldn't have trusted you!" I yelled at him, biding my time until I could try to run.

"Eden, you have to understand, I really was trying to get you home. They're going to kill me. Slowly and painfully." I tuned him out, thinking it was an excuse, until he said the magic words. "Tony and Santos described in great detail how they'd do it, and now I've fucked up. I promise I'll do what I can to get you home." He swallowed and went silent, but from what I could tell in the dash lights, he had paled considerably.

"I don't trust you. I only *marginally* believe you. And I want a fucking knife like you promised." When he pointed at the glove compartment, I popped it open to find one in a tactical sheath, and bonus, it was small enough to replace the one from my boot.

"Put your seatbelt on," he demanded, urgency in his voice. I pulled it over me and clicked it into its latch, but it didn't matter. The roadblock prevented us from taking the exit we needed to turn around. Its mere presence said it all. "He knew I'd run with you." He turned his head to glance at me for just a moment as he put on his turn signal. "Do whatever you need to to survive until I can get you out. Do you understand?"

Oh, I understood alright. I understood that I was fucked, but so was he. What I didn't understand was why he had such an interest in my well-being. I mean, the guys could be a big part of it, but he'd pretty much shown his disdain early on for the mafia Families in general, and the Carlotti men in particular. I didn't trust this about-face he seemed to have done.

"I'm not making any promises. Besides, Rodrigo will kill me on sight. He probably just wants to do it himself for his personal satisfaction, to make sure I stay dead this time."

Fields didn't answer me, but really, there wasn't much else to say on the subject.

fifteen

monsters

Tony

"**W**hy isn't she back yet?" Santos' question echoed the one that had been floating around my head for the last several hours. "We would have heard something by now if anything happened, right?"

My shrug didn't seem to be what he was looking for since he cursed and stomped out of my office. As soon as I was fairly certain he was out of earshot, I picked up my phone and called my father.

"Where is she?" I demanded as soon as he picked up.

"Is that any way to greet your father, Antonio?"

His avoidance pissed me off, and I had to restrain myself from shouting into the speaker. "She should have been back hours ago. What did you have her doing?" He sighed, sounding tired, but we were all fucking tired. This shit had worn on everyone, and his continual insistence on putting Eden in the middle was nearly intolerable. I wasn't going to stand for it any longer. "Call her in. She's done. This was never her fight, and I want her out."

"Antonio, you've been left out of the planning for a reason. I'll let you know when I have an update." He didn't wait for a response before he hung up on me. And that wasn't going to stand either. It was time for him to step aside like he'd been planning to do before Rodrigo's defection.

"Vanni!" I shouted, knowing he'd hear me. His room had been uncustomarily quiet all day. None of us were dealing very well with Eden playing bait, especially after last night, and I still couldn't believe she'd gone today in spite of it. If it were anyone else, I'd call it a straight-up betrayal, but I'd just cussed her out and walked off when she reminded me that she'd already agreed prior to the night's events. I'd had enough of the fucking short leash the ankle monitors had us on; it was time to rectify that issue...and several others.

Marco

When Eden got back, I was going to beat her ass for scaring us, then I was locking her in her room and fucking *daring* Uncle Vinnie to send her out again. He needed a few things explained to him, and if Tony didn't handle it soon, I would.

To keep from driving the others up the wall with my observations and questions, I'd retreated to the game room to kill some time. The crack of the cue ball hitting the set I'd racked was as harsh as my mood, but as I lined up my next shot, I swore the scent that was purely Eden wafted up from the felt.

It was a mix of her, the shower products she used, and the light perfume she'd taken to wearing while she was gone. And right then, despite the time we'd had the last few weeks, I wished she'd stayed gone until Rodrigo and his ilk were six feet under so she wouldn't be in the middle of this mess. Being apart from her would be hard, but I'd even sacrifice the memories we'd made in this very room. I knew we'd have christened Tony's pool table at one point or another anyway, and the rest...I'd have made damn sure that happened regardless of where we were.

I finished potting the balls and had a smoke to calm myself down as I made my plans. Tony and I were about to have a talk about Eden and Uncle Vinnie. Our girl was coming home and staying home. Fuck anyone that thought differently.

Eden

R odrigo did not, in fact, kill me on sight. He slapped me hard enough that I thought he might have broken my cheekbone, spitting out that it was repayment for Santos clocking him on my behalf, but he didn't kill me. No, his machinations went beyond that. He'd decided that death, even a slow one, was too easy for me. And for his son's betrayal. Fields' words played in my head, the ones about surviving at any cost, but I was afraid that cost might be too high.

Maybe it would be better if I removed myself from the situation before my mind, and likely body, cracked under whatever retribution Rodrigo had planned. I'd have to wait and play it by ear; I wouldn't leave the guys for anything, but they were still tormented over my past mistreatment at Rodrigo's hands, and their parts in it. I could only imagine how they'd feel if I went through an undetermined amount of time in my captor's possession only to have what was left of my broken remains delivered to them. A shudder worked through me at the thought that it could be in pieces. I liked to think of myself as strong, but I'd had a taste of torture...I didn't relish a prolonged repeat of that scenario.

My racing thoughts and contingency plans were brought to a halt when Rodrigo slapped his hand on Danny's old desk. It was surreal to be back in his office, especially while knowing he was gone, but seeing the man who was the catalyst for nearly every bad thing in my life taking over the seedy haven I'd found when I'd had nowhere else to go was hard to swallow. It also didn't help that I'd died in one of the backrooms of the club. I'd kinda always thought that might happen, but in those imaginings, it had been from an overdose or at the hands of an overenthusiastic john, not from being caught in the middle of a power grab.

"Are you listening to me, you little whore?" he demanded, voice rising with his irritation. Staring at a point past his shoulder, I nodded. I couldn't stand to look at the man. "I don't think you are. I think you're biding your time, waiting on a rescue from your not-so-white knights. You might think that will happen, but let me show you why you're going to make sure they don't come near my club." While he opened a laptop, this one newer than the one Danny used to have, he continued with his warning. "If they step foot into my territory, this will be sent to the DA and the news stations. I'm sure you're well aware that I have control of the local police, so I don't think you want them going back there. And with all of this, it's only a matter of time before I have every judge or official under my thumb that was dumb enough to dip a toe out of line near Danny and his propensity for recording it ."

I blanched at what was playing on the screen when he flipped it around with a smug ass smile. But he ceased to exist for me as I watched a younger version of myself clean up a room with Sam, my fear and upset plain on my pale face. I continued to watch the video as we loaded up plastic totes with the grisly remains that had been made into more manageable pieces, knowing that I was fucked if it ever got out.

"H-how did you get this? He promised there was no record of it." My whisper was quiet, but without sound on the video, Rodrigo heard me just fine.

"Oh, Eden, you think that's all he lied about? Here, watch." He reached around and clicked a key, then little thumbnails of videos popped up on the screen.

I was in so many of them, doing so many *very* illegal things. Things that the statute of limitations wasn't up on, I was sure. But worse than that was who else was in those insurance videos that Danny had accumulated over the years. I didn't care about myself so much; it just cemented my certainty that I wasn't long for this plane of existence. While I was sad that I'd miss out on so much of my life now that I'd straightened it out, I accepted it. What I couldn't accept, and what Rodrigo was going to exploit, were the clips with the guys in them, namely Tony and Vanni. I was passed out in Vanni's arms, and Tony's arm was frozen part way up with a gun in his hand. I hadn't known the exact details, but I did know that if I hit play, Tony would be finishing his act of murdering Sam. *I'm so fucking screwed.*

"You see, you're going to do exactly as I say, when I say it, and before you think you can get your hands on the hard copies, just know I've uploaded them all to my own personally developed cloud. The Carlotti Family shouldn't have fucked with me. This regime change was always coming, but the fact that they took a whore's side, that my only *child* took your side? They're all going to regret it. It could have been peaceful; Santos could have been at my side, working with the Carlottis, married off to one of their women to join us together. Letting Danny and the other hustlers run the neutral zone was a waste of potential, a mistake. Old man Finelli is just as much at fault for leaving an area to fester with the frustrations of the tit-for-tat skirmishes and unnecessary deaths each side dealt the other despite the truce the Families put in place. I'm preventing what would have been an all-out war that would have torn the city apart, and probably further, especially once the authorities got involved. This isn't quite how I planned it, but I can make it work." He shrugged as he finished his diatribe. The man was a great criminal. He had the mindset and ambition down, and he'd maneuvered each piece of his real-life game board into place, minus a few recalcitrant ones. It appeared I was the major wrench in his plans. Coming back as I had, my fault or not, had caused a rift with his son, and now we were going to be used as an example of what happened when he was crossed. As far as coups went, it was brilliant. As one of those persons on the opposite end of the victors, it sucked ass.

"What's the plan then, Rodrigo? Torment the guys, get whatever concessions you can from the Carlottis as a whole, and then turn me loose?" I scoffed at the idea that I'd be allowed to leave while breathing. My thumb subconsciously moved to my birthmark, rubbing it for comfort, and the motion wasn't lost on Rodrigo.

"Something like that, minus letting you go. Might send a warning, starting with that blemish my son copied, if you give me any trouble." He nodded at my wrist, and I covered it with my palm as if that could protect it. "For now, you can get over here and let me see if there's any use left to you." I didn't understand or move quickly enough, so he snapped his fingers, pointing to the floor behind his desk. "Now, bitch!"

I scurried out of the chair and reluctantly walked around the desk, pausing a foot away until his glare warned me to close the gap. He jerked my skirt up, fully exposing me to his gaze, then shoved his hand between my legs until I widened them and stared at a spot on the wall behind him. I couldn't believe this was what it had come to. All those years of pain and misery, only to be right back at square one.

My heart steeled itself as he forced one finger in, then another a moment later.

"Not as cherry as it once was, but it seems to have recovered nicely from my associate's foray into going off-script. You don't happen to know which one did it, do you?" he asked, curiosity rampant in voice and expression. He chuckled at my lack of response in both regards, then jammed his fingers harder against me. "The cop that had his fun with this," another wiggle of fingers had me gritting my teeth, "was tracked down and taken out, just like his partner, but Evans had himself torn a new asshole, *literally*, before he died. That kind of retribution only comes from someone that felt personally slighted, but I haven't been able to determine who it was yet. I figured one of them would have told you by now." He shrugged, as he seemed to do often, like it was his own personal tic, and removed his hand from between my legs. He made a point of wiping his fingers on my scrap of a skirt before he snapped them and pointed down at the floor.

When he spread his legs, I allowed myself one solitary tear that I hid behind my curtain of tangled hair as I knelt down and prepared to let my mind drift to anything other than what I was doing. "Bite me like you did my man earlier tonight, and I'll pull all of your teeth out and send them to Antonio," he threatened as he unfastened his pants and pulled his flaccid dick out.

With a shudder of revulsion that he probably took as a tremble of fear, I parted my lips and sucked him in to the hilt, hard and without preamble, before drawing back to roll the soft head around my tongue. He thickened, growing until he filled my mouth, and I had to adjust to avoid hitting him with my teeth. I hadn't lost them to the drugs, and I wasn't about to lose them to this dick now.

As he palmed the back of my head and moaned, he sprawled back in the office chair, making it squeak with every pump of his hips. I had barely set my pace with monotonous, repetitive motions that I hoped would eventually get him off, when there was a knock at the door.

"Enter," Rodrigo called out above me as he held my head down, burying my nose in his graying pubes until I couldn't breathe.

The door opened, and a man's chuckle followed my desperate gasps for air when Rodrigo finally let me up.

"So you really did get her," a vaguely familiar voice mused, "and you didn't waste any time putting her to use, I see."

Rodrigo fisted my hair, using it to pull me up and

twist my head so I could see who was getting a show at my expense. I didn't give two shits about someone watching, unless it was the guys, but if my reaction was what he'd been after, he got it when my eyes landed on Peter Finelli. My shocked stare lasted an instant before curses poured from my lips.

"You motherfucking traitorous piece of shit!" The smack was immediate, as was the coppery tang of blood where my molars had cut into my cheek.

"That's not what your mouth is for, whore," Rodrigo snapped at me before shoving my head back into his crotch. I was fucking pissed I had an open cut in my mouth when I knew he planned on jizzing in it. *If I catch something from this bastard...*

"She's a feisty one, isn't she?" Peter asked, amusement lacing his tone. "You plan on passing her around? I wouldn't mind taking a turn after what I saw in the video. Have to admit, those Carlotti boys tore that shit up." Peter's speech pattern was quick, too quick, and from what I remembered, he wasn't that excitable. Made me wonder if he'd been dipping into his own product instead of just peddling it. If Edward Finelli's son had thrown his lot in with Rodrigo, he was unpredictable enough, but add in drugs, and I could be fucked in more than one way. And at least one way was already on the table as far as Rodrigo was concerned.

He never slowed the pace he was forcing on me as he told Peter to go for it. "Actually, stick it in her ass. I haven't decided whether I'm going to breed the bitch or not. Wouldn't that be a grand 'fuck you' to my ungrateful child? Getting his whore pregnant and replacing him..." Rodrigo cackled at his twisted idea, and my stomach curdled at the thought of him fucking me, let alone *impregnating* me.

That was not how I wanted to end up being a mother, if at all. I was afraid it would break Santos, not to mention what it would mean for everything else. Hell, if I didn't wind up dead, it would be a line in the sand that I wasn't sure we would be able to overcome. And no matter *who* the father was, I would never willingly leave my own child with a psychopathic rapist. I'd run with it first, then deal with the fallout later.

"Get her up on the desk, if you don't mind, DeLuca." Peter's comment was accompanied by the jangle of his belt as he unfastened it.

Rodrigo grunted, sounding eerily like his son when he did that, and hauled me off of his spit-shined dick. He snapped his fingers at me, and I didn't bother stalling. I wanted to get it over with, so I climbed onto the desk after scooting his laptop off to the side.

It was uncomfortable as fuck with the edge of the desk digging into the back of my neck, but I let my head fall back, giving me the chance to see inside the drawer Rodrigo stored the laptop in. The one where Danny kept all kinds of miscellaneous shit, including the concealed compartment that held all of his USB drives. It was currently open, contents intact. I'd bet anything that Rodrigo had only recently figured out how to get into it and was still going through the thousands of hours of footage Danny had kept. His earlier reference to black-mailing influential men made me sure I was correct. If I could get my hands on those, it would take care of half of my problems, letting me take his ass out sooner than later.

"Condoms and lubricant, if you want them, are in that jar over there. Ol' Danny Boy had them everywhere, though it's mostly down to the cherry-flavored shit. Man sure did like his theme," Rodrigo drawled as he pressed his dick against my lips, demanding entry.

I opened up to take him in, nearly gagging as he used the new angle to shove straight into my tonsils. Peter made some comment about easy access and my piercings when Rodrigo commanded me to lift my legs and exposed my lack of underwear. I was too busy trying to breathe since Rodrigo had decided to fold me in half, using the backs of my knees as hand-holds as he railed my throat.

A squirt of liquid hit my asshole before Peter started to press in, not taking much time to let me adjust nor caring that it fucking burned like a bitch. To top it off, I was going to have a cherry-flavored ass and the discomfort that came from using the shit.

Fucking Danny. Even dead, the prick was still a pain in my ass. *Literally.*

As Rodrigo throbbed and came in my mouth, forcing me to swallow his cum, I promised myself to end both of the violating fucks as soon as I could. Preferably without taking out myself and those I cared about in the process. When he pulled out, my jaw and neck screamed from the strain, and the swelling cut inside my cheek throbbed like a sick bird's ass.

"You really plan on getting her pregnant? She made Danny a pretty penny shaking her ass and turning tricks in the backrooms. Hate to lose out on all that revenue, you know?" Peter's speech was interspersed with soft grunts and heavy breathing from his exertions. He wouldn't quit fucking playing with my piercings either, and I despised that it was marginally turning me on. Thankfully, my biological response was tempered by the utter disgust I held for the man. As he sped up, my body jerked with every thrust, the only thing keeping me from sliding off the other end was where I'd hooked my hands under my raised ass to grip the edge of the desk.

"Maybe," came Rodrigo's reply from the office chair he'd flopped back in when he was finished with me. A click of a lighter, then the pungent smoke of one of Danny's prized cigars filled my nose. I'd kept my eyes closed, making it easier to pretend I wasn't getting fucked in the ass by a Finelli again. Ironic how it had come full circle since the night that Tony and Vanni had carted me out of there.

"I haven't decided yet if I'd rather do that or let the whole crew at her. I'd film it for my son and those Carlotti fucks before sending her back in pieces for a Christmas surprise. She'd keep in the freezer." He said it so nonchalantly that I knew I had limited time to figure shit out.

I didn't want to die like that, or at all, really, but the thought of the guys having to watch it all go down was more than unpalatable; it was fucking horrendous. I'd go nuts if I had to see it happen to them.

I desperately feared that Rodrigo's threats would be my fate if I couldn't destroy his evidence or escape with my men. Finally, the hot, lashing burn of the degenerate emptying into me came. As did a slap to my ass when he pulled out amidst a rush of liquid indicating the cheap condom had broken, deeply searing in the shame that I'd been with three men that weren't mine in a single night. Not to mention my own broken promise widening the fissures in my soul after ending up back here when I'd sworn I wouldn't. I wouldn't even be in my current predicament had I listened and stayed home, but no, I had to live up to my promises to Vinnie, and now it could take everything from me.

After I dragged myself, stiff and sore from the night's events, off of the desk and straightened my clothes the best I could, Rodrigo let me leave. Unfortunately, he had me escorted to Danny's old apartment within the club. I was to stay in the bedroom and wait for him. Wanting their mess off of me, I used the shower then huddled on the bed in a t-shirt I'd found in a drawer. Needing to escape instead of dwelling on what had just transpired, I brought last night's memory to the forefront of my mind, hiding in the happiness it evoked while hoping it wouldn't be the last one to do so.

sixteen

darkside

Eden

Last Night

"You need to give it a rest, Tony. I'm going. It's what I came back to do, and I need to see it through. I put your father off for a week after you all had your say." I didn't want to fucking go as it was, and he was just making it worse.

I hadn't even broken the news to anyone else yet. Tony only knew because I'd come up to his office to ask if he wanted lunch, and Vinnie had happened to call while I was in there. There was little point in trying to hide that I had a second phone after Santos saw it, but I hadn't been carrying it around like I was today. Vinnie had messaged earlier that he'd be calling, and when he didn't do so by mid-morning, I'd stuck it in my pocket. Now Tony was pissed that I wouldn't tell him any particulars, and Vinnie wasn't too happy I hadn't made myself available for his call or taken it in private.

"The fuck I'll let it go, Eden. *Never again!* I did once, and hated it. You going out for whatever cat and mouse game my father is playing is done. Do you understand me? The longer we let it go on, the worse it's going to get, and I'm not letting him risk you anymore. We can't lose you again, dammit!"

"No one is losing anyone, Antonio! I've been fine; Vinnie agreed to make sure I was well guarded, or I wouldn't have gone in the first place. Current events don't have any bearing on what happened back then either. The situation is completely different." Jesus, the man was nearly apoplectic and all over a day out shopping. It wasn't any different than any other time.

"I know we're not because you're not going. And it has *everything* to do with the past. Had we not found you in the club, Rodrigo wouldn't have put a hit out on you! If he hadn't been a sleazy fuck over his son's girlfriend, you wouldn't have had to leave in the first place."

"Tony, we have no idea what would have happened in the years in between even if I'd stayed. It's ridiculous to daydream about that. I did it for years, but it doesn't do anyone any good. I'll concede the rest because it happened, but I have to believe that Vinnie has a plan to fix all of this. He hasn't remained a force to be reckoned with all this time without having a clue." The conversation didn't seem to be so much about the now but the fear of the past repeating itself. While I understood his feelings, I couldn't stand to live trapped or a half-life anymore. I was ready to be free, goddamnit.

"Oh, I know what would have happened. Santos would have married his high-school sweetheart while the rest of us were jealous as fuck, forced to make damn sure you only thought of us as brothers, so we didn't break his heart or ours."

And now I was just plain pissed. "Well, you all had a fucking great way of showing that brotherly affection, Tony! I don't think you're comprehending that painting me a pretty picture of what my life *should* have been like is just fucking cruel since I wallowed in the shitty pits of this city for all those years instead! So, please, tell me again how you felt about it." I'd turned my back on him, not wanting him to see how vulnerable I was at the moment, but his shout had me spinning back to face him.

"We were all in love, or halfway there, with you *years* ago! You weren't the only one that suffered, Eden!" He just couldn't leave well enough alone.

"So what? You think that I should just let it go? After everything I've been through?" My voice cracked at the end, the fury and bitterness that I usually kept well and buried surfacing to wreak havoc on my composure.

"Isn't that exactly what you're expecting us to

do?" he demanded, a bit softer after taking in my expression. I deflated at that. "We were *all* mistaken. We were all victims if you want to get technical. Now we can do something about it, and while we can't erase what happened or go back in time, we *can* choose how we proceed now."

That was all well and good, but there was something more I had to know now that he'd broached the subject. "What would you have done if I'd gone to you? Any of you? Would you have believed me?"

His hesitation didn't last long, but it was enough to shutter my heart to stop the pain from leaking out. I must not have hidden that, or the uncontrollable hardening of my expression gave me away.

"Yes, I would have. We all would have." He sighed, and I knew what he did. *They might not have.* "Look, Eden, we were barely adults ourselves, and despite the lifestyle we grew up in, we weren't savvy on the dating world outside of sticking our dicks in willing pussy. Even you have to admit that, except for Santos, we were pushy horndogs."

He wasn't wrong, but he also wasn't right. Santos got plenty of action; he just hadn't pushed *me* for it and had been content to fool around until I was ready for more. But I didn't think it was quite the time to bring that up or risk getting sidetracked. I wasn't sure if we'd end up arguing over a different topic, or if the sexual tension that always simmered between me and the guys would burst into an inferno and take us away into a burning heap of lust.

"But you'd have taken Rodrigo's side. *Family* first, isn't that right?" He scowled at my finger quotations, though he kept on track with his answer.

"Sure, at first we might have. Hell, until he pulled that shit, you would have questioned it yourself. He was always a good dad to Santos, and he was good enough at his job to get into his position. But all of us would have at least *asked,* and I don't think your mother could have helped herself if she was that intent on keeping you away. It looked bad, Eden, really bad. At first, I thought maybe you didn't come back because something more happened between you and Santos, but the guy was distraught."

A frown pulled at his lips and dipped his brows together as if he were remembering a younger, more broken version of Santos. What he looked like in the transition from a sweet boy to the jaggedly healed asshole he had been when we reunited. I imagined it closely resembled the same one I'd gone through, and while I wasn't covered in quite so many physical scars, some days, my jagged pieces barely fit inside me without bleeding me out on the floor with every breath I took. But there was one thing I knew for sure, even back then.

"If you mean rape, Santos could never have done that. He wasn't, *isn't,* his father." I was adamant on that fact, and no matter how many shitty things he'd done since then, that wasn't one that was in his repertoire.

Surprise lit Tony's face as his brows reached for his hairline. "Look at you defending him. Thought you were still pissed he threatened to lock you up after you got all cozy in the garage?" A noncommittal grunt was all he got in response, which earned a small chuckle, but then he got serious again. "My other fear was that you ended up pregnant, or worse, and that's why you didn't come back. I have to say I felt like an incompetent idiot when I found out you'd never left the city, but that was on your mother as well. She made it sound like you were long gone, and you weren't anywhere we thought to look." He winced when he realized what he'd said. "I can only apologize, Eden, that we didn't turn the city over to find you. We would have brought you home or figured something else out if you didn't want to stay here."

Anger seeped back, but not at the homeless-stripper-cum-drugged-up-whore references he was dancing around. "See, Tony, that's where I have trouble with this. You all *did* let me go. While you all may have been hurt and felt betrayed, and maybe Santos had it a bit worse, *I* was the one that paid the price for *everything* while you all went on with your lives. Your *luxurious* lives. Fuck, I'm so far down on the totem pole even your servants have a better grasp on your lifestyle. Me? I couldn't even find a fucking television, and I sucked your brother's dick in an effort to let me out so I could run. And you know what I'd have directly gone and done?" From the crossed arms, narrowed eyes, and scowling lips, he already knew what I'd have done. But I needed to drive that home. "As soon as I'd gotten my fix, I'd have jumped the first bus, train, or fucking truck driver on their way out of town and continued to use my pussy as currency until I felt I'd gotten far enough away that you'd never find where I'd gone. Just like you originally thought."

"Fuck you, Eden. You want to lash out, tell me how awful it was? Go ahead. But don't put words in my mouth that I never even thought of. If it had occurred to me that you'd have gone that route, we'd have checked every scuz hole and strip joint rather than looking in shelters for a scared girl or back-end alleys for a dead body. The best we could hope for was that we'd find it quickly enough to be identified so there would at least be some fucking closure!"

"Wait, what?" *They'd thought I was dead?* Maybe they had mentioned or insinuated it before, but I wasn't recollecting that conversation.

"Every unclaimed body that could have possibly been yours was viewed at the morgue. We bribed every shelter operator to let us know if they saw you, and Santos was haggard enough from not sleeping that they believed him when he said he only wanted you safe. We searched dumpsters, and I personally had a talk with anyone I knew connected to trafficking. You. Were. Gone. Either you got on a bus or train, and we couldn't track you, or you'd hitched a ride with someone. We had no choice but to let you go. My father was ready for me to take on more in my role, I needed to choose who would be at my side for that, and Santos needed somewhere to direct his anger. I'll spare you any further details, but I'm sure you can figure it out." He was right; I knew exactly how that had turned out, but he was still scowling at me like it was my fault.

"And now I'm here. We all suffered and survived, I get it. Really, I do, it's just somewhat hard to swallow that mine was a hell of a lot less glamorous than all of yours, but that's my issue to get over, not anyone else's. And now that we've both had our say on the past, I need another answer. Everyone else has said what they want, in one way or another, but you haven't." I bit my lip, uncertain of how he'd respond. Before today, I'd have said he was onboard, but the offhand comments didn't mean that was how things were going to be.

"I want it all, Eden, but that doesn't mean I'll get it. We'll have to see how it all plays out. There are too many variables that could change the outcome," he evaded, which made me lose my temper. Fuck him and his *variables*.

"What exactly are you proposing, Antonio? That I be your house whore? Date all of you? Or will you draw straws to see who I get the privilege to be with?" I knew I was being a bitch, but I wanted answers, and pushing him to the point of losing his temper, and subsequently, his restraint, was hard to do while keeping it civil.

"Santos is as much my family as Vanni and Marco are, and he's my closest friend. If he prefers I step aside, I'll do so." From the stiff set to his shoulders and gritted teeth, I didn't think that was quite how he felt on the subject, but I figured a few more pokes would have him blowing his top. At least I wasn't afraid he'd off me anymore. No, it was more likely he'd get off *on* me these days.

A vision of him jacking off on my tits while he held me down by my throat flitted through my head a half-second before a streak of heat did the same quite a bit lower. It nearly distracted me from my agenda, but I had plans for it to end somewhat like that anyhow. I looked forward to breaking the man that stood before me.

"And what if Santos isn't the only one I want? What if Vanni and Marco *won't* step aside? You two besties gonna go circle jerk it together? Well, actually, that's probably not enough for a circle," I mused as Tony's cheeks faintly colored up. He wasn't fair enough for a true flush, but I was definitely under his skin now. "Or I could just say fuck all of you and leave. For good this time. No phone, no fake I.D., nothing for you to hold over my head." I crossed my arms and cocked a hip out, determined to stand my ground until he gave it up.

"Not happening. Pick one," he demanded with a glare.

"Uh, pick one, what? I literally just told you I don't want just *one* of you." I was confused and didn't like that he'd found a way around answering me. I'd for sure thought I had him this time. When he whipped his phone out and rapidly started texting, I got downright pissed. "Excuse me, I wasn't done! You're not ignoring me, Antonio."

A quirk of a brow and the devilish glint in his eyes were my only warning that he'd cooked up something I wasn't going to like. "Do you want the traditional hoopla with a white dress, or will a Justice of the Peace suffice?"

"Huh?" *He's lost his damn mind. Good going, Eden. You broke him, alright, just not in the good way.* Seriously, I could fuck up a wet dream if you gave me long enough.

"A wedding, Eden, keep up. Mama will probably insist on a celebration when she comes back home, but I'll let you choose the ceremony if you want one, and of course, which one of us you'd rather be with." He didn't even look up from his screen as he spouted his nonsense.

"What the fuck are you talking about? For one, I've never even *met* your mother, so why would she want to throw a party for me? And what in the actual *fuck* are you going on about because it sure as hell sounds like you're planning a wedding!"

"Shotgun wedding if you want to get technical, Eden, though it's traditionally the man who's being held accountable. Now, whose name do you want? Carlotti or DeLuca? Maybe I could get Santos to change his last name, so it won't matter," he muttered when I stood silent in disbelief.

"I'm not *marrying* anyone, Antonio. Practical jokes are Marco's and Vanni's schtick, so what are you playing at?" I was plain irate at being ignored and worried I was about to be shanghaied into a marriage I wasn't at all prepared for.

"Oh, there will be a wedding, Eden," he hissed, eyes narrowed as he slipped his phone into the pocket of his slacks before advancing on me. "And there will be a marriage license signed and filed before midnight tonight. Now... Pick. One."

My feet hauled ass before my mind was made up to run for the door. I got it open and shrieked for the one I assumed could talk the crazy man off the ledge. This was *not* what I'd had in mind. "*Santos!* Get your ass in here!" I didn't manage more before I was yanked back and dragged to Tony's desk, where he bent me over until my cheek rested on the cool, polished top.

"Santos it is then," he all but growled in my ear. With one hand pinning me down by my neck, his hips snug enough against mine that I could feel the growing length of his dick, he pulled his phone back out. "Congratulations, Mrs. DeLuca. You're officially a part of the family. *And your ass isn't going anywhere!* Don't you *ever* fucking threaten to leave again, understood?!"

All I could do was blink in shock until my mouth ran away with itself. "You seem to be missing a few things, Tony, like a lick of fucking sense." I took his grunt as him waiting for me to further enlighten him. "For one, you don't have a shotgun, so you can't exactly call it a *shotgun* wedding, and I don't know... How about *consent?* Now, get off me, you fucking asshole, so I can kick you in those big ass brass balls you seem to think you're packing."

I missed whatever he started to say as Santos burst through the door, rage and worry twisting his lips and scars alike into a mask of living violence. "What the fuck, Tony? Let her go. Now."

But Tony had no intention of letting me loose. "There's the groom now," he replied, completely ignoring the threat. "And I can get a shotgun if you'd like, Eden. But make no mistake, your signature *will* be on that license as soon as the courier arrives with it."

Half a step away, Santos came to a halt and reached for Tony, intent on removing him. Through the curtain of hair hanging in my face, I could see his confusion. "Let her go, Tony, and tell me what's going on in here before I kick your ass." When he pulled on

Tony's arm, the crazy-ass man curled it around my neck and yanked me up with him, twisting to use me as a shield.

Annoyed at being manhandled, I filled Santos in after blowing wayward strands of hair out of my face. "Your boss here has lost his ever-loving mind and has decided we're getting married. Me and you, not me and him." To punctuate my irritation, I kicked my captor in the shin, barely earning a grunt in return.

"He's *what?* Tony, man, what the fuck?" *Yep, that's the consensus. A whole lot of fucks, just not the one I was aiming for.*

"She said she was leaving. Now, she's not. Problem solved," he delivered succinctly. And then it was Santos' turn to glare at me.

"I did not," I argued, preempting the accusation that was surely about to come from him. It would echo the one he held in his hard gaze as he stared me down. "I said if he wanted to make my decisions for me, I could just leave. That, apparently, was his cue to get even more high-handed and resulted in this mess."

"You don't want to marry me? You were going to leave?" *Oh, fuck me in the ass,* he's *butthurt now?*

It did result in Tony's arms relaxing around me enough that I slipped away; he stopped playing my shadow when I only perched on his desk instead of heading for the door. Like a sane person would. Tony's phone buzzed in the lull, and when he looked at the message, a scowl took over his features once more.

"You want her to keep her maiden name or not?"

"Yes!" came from me at the same time as Santos declared his vehement "No!"

"Excuse me?!" At the unrelenting stares, I threw my hands up in the air. "You know, now I understand exactly how you two are BFFs. You're both fucking nuts. Absolutely goddamned cuckoo for cocoa puffs and certified batshit crazy! No one else would put up with you two. It's like a defense mechanism...attract the lunatic or some shit. Thank fuck it isn't catching."

Thank god that Vanni and Marco chose that moment to come through the open door. "Hey, what's—"

"Going on?" I cut him off. At his nod, I hurried to fill him in, indicating Santos and Tony respectively, just in case the insanity *was* catching. "Nutjob just joined crackpot's lovely idea to marry me off. To him." My finger landed squarely on Santos, who had the grace to cringe a bit. "And before they start, I did *not* say I was leaving. I said I *could* if the mob boss in training here wanted to make my decisions for me. I won't live in a goddamned dictatorship!" I got it all out, glaring at Tony before he could open his smug ass mouth, but he just stood there with a smirk like I was digging my own hole. And from their reactions...I had. *Fuck my life. Wet dreams, Eden. Wet. Dreams.*

"Why would you threaten it if you weren't considering it?" Marco demanded.

But it was Vanni's face falling before he steeled it and stalked out without a word that had me reconsidering my words. Not that I was sure what the fuck else I could have said that would have gotten through Tony's thick head. I just wished things had gone in a different direction because, as it stood, if I went through with Tony's plans, I was about to lose three of them.

But I couldn't deal with that at the moment. I had to go after Vanni, especially after all the time we'd spent together lately and the declarations we'd made. Yeah, I'd fucked up, royally. Now I had to go own up to it.

"*Fuck!*" I hopped off the desk and stalked the few steps to Tony, poking him in the chest with each word. "Had you just said you'd commit, you asshole, none of this would be happening right now. Just fucking pull that stick out of your ass for once and say what you actually want." I whirled on my heel and addressed the other two. "Santos, if you wanted to propose, that was a shitty way to do it, and Marco, I love you, please...sort these two out while I go grovel?" Marco quirked his brow, acting his normal self, but I could see the worry under his usual devil-may-care mien. I lifted up on my tip-toes to give him a brief kiss on my way out the door.

"Got it, Edie," he said with a wink, but he

grabbed my arm when I was halfway out in the hall. "Fair warning, if you ever did try? I'd lock your sweet ass in the basement." As I blinked, trying to come up with a suitable reassurance, or any words at all, he turned me loose, smacking my ass with the order to "Go find Vanni. I'll rub your jaw better later."

I just nodded, not even a bit surprised he suggested giving Vanni a blowjob, but I knew it would take more than me choking on his dick to reassure him that I wasn't leaving...although it couldn't hurt to try.

seventeen

marry you

Eden

Last Night

I finally found Vanni out on the back porch, smoking a joint. I almost commented about a piss test, but I was sure he and Marco had it covered, so I dove right into the apology.

"Hey, you know I wouldn't leave, right?" He barely turned his head to glance at me before staring off into the distance. "Dammit, Vanni, I'm fucking sorry, okay? I *wouldn't* leave you. Not willingly."

He passed the joint before answering me, and I took a heavy hit of the earthy smoke, holding it until the urge to cough had passed.

"I made you a promise, Edie—if you wanted to go and even keep *me* from finding you, I'd make it happen. The possibility of that coming to pass, no matter how minute, fucking hurts, but I'll keep my word if you need it." Fucker was going to break my heart with his martyr ass.

"Nope, not leaving, just proving a point to your thick-headed brother. When he got all high-handed and started acting like everything he'd said before didn't mean squat, I got a little pissed. Now I'm apparently getting hitched. How do you feel about dating a married woman, Vanni?" My teasing got a wan smile, but as I passed the joint back, it faded.

"Actually, I'm kind of bummed it's not me, but between Tony and Santos, I knew I never stood a chance if you decided to go that route. Doesn't mean my feelings have changed or that I plan to step aside." He shrugged as he took a last pull and crushed the end out in an ashtray on the ledge.

Relief coursed through me, but before I could articulate that, he pulled me to him and tipped his face down to cover my lips with his. I was confused when he opened his mouth over mine, but his hands cupped my cheeks to keep me in place. Then he exhaled, filling my lungs with the heady smoke.

A thrill of need pulsed through me at the unexpected move that was somehow highly erotic yet still perfectly intimate. I stood there, staring into the dark depths of Vanni's eyes while clinging to his biceps as I blew it back out.

"I see you two made up just fine," Marco intoned from the doorway.

"I think we did?" I answered while simultaneously questioning Vanni. He nodded and hugged me to him, my back to his chest and his chin resting on my head. I really loved the feeling of being snuggled back into the warmth his body offered in the cooling afternoon air.

"Good," Marco began, coming out to join us, "because I need to ask you something before you make any decisions." Then the fucker dropped down and held out a ring. "Eden Moretti, will you marry us?"

Although Vanni had stiffened, he instantly relaxed again at the 'us' part while I stared at the big lug in front of me. What else could I say but yes? Seemed there was a consensus on the matter anyhow, not that I was opposed to it in general, but I hadn't imagined it would be *now*.

"Well, if I'm going to have your spawn one day, I suppose we should do it up proper, amirite?" I winked at him and held out my hand as he chuckled, taking the pretty solitaire from its bed of black velvet.

"Uh, Edie, just to clarify, you do mean *all* of us, yes?" Vanni asked from behind, holding on to me just a smidge too tightly until I nodded my head under his chin. "Then I'm good with it, but you'll have to decide who it will be on paper. Even the Carlottis can't get away with a group marriage, not legally anyway." His head dipped to the side to nip at my neck before sucking at the sensitive skin while Marco slipped the ring on my finger amidst my faint moan of delight. Leave it to fucking Marco to know my ring size; even I didn't know that shit.

"Marco! You fucker! When did you go ring shopping?" Tony barged out onto the porch, bringing his thundercloud with him.

"The day she left," he popped off with a smirk. "I may have followed her for a while to make sure she made it out of the city. Right before I turned around, a billboard for a jeweler caught my eye, and I decided I'd be prepared for when she came back." He winked at me just as I had moments ago, defusing my urge to call him a stalker.

"Well, you might get your wish, asshole. Santos is refusing to do it," Tony grumbled, staring at me guardedly like I wasn't going to like what else he might say.

But I was crushed and didn't care to hear anything else. It was stupid to be upset after my own reaction earlier, but to know Santos didn't actually want me made my chest constrict with emotion. The pain was bad enough that I couldn't tell if it was causing my ribs to rebel or if that was my heart turning to ash.

"Guess it's settled then," I managed, pulling against Vanni's hold, desperately wanting to get out from under their scrutiny and into the privacy of my room before I broke. I latched on to a somewhat plausible excuse when he didn't let go. "I want a smoke, Vanni. Let up, will you?" He slowly loosened his arms, and I slipped free, refusing to make eye contact with anyone as I made a beeline straight upstairs.

The first tear fell as I opened my door, but when I threw it shut behind me, it bounced back. Marco had followed me. *I'm such a fucking bitch. He just proposed, and I took off, butthurt that Santos rejected me.*

"Marco, I'm sorry. I didn't mean to be rude, or what I said, not like that." Tears tracked down my cheeks and clogged my throat, preventing me from explaining myself further.

"I know you didn't, Edie, but I'm not leaving you upset on your wedding day. I'm positive there's more to it than that. Santos has been a fucking pill since you left; there's no way he doesn't want you." He advanced on me, folding me into a hug as I let my emotions out. Marco made soothing rumbles that were probably words while he held me, but I was too distraught to make them out.

Past and present hurts collided to form a storm of snot and tears until I'd exhausted myself and felt seriously self-conscious standing there in the middle of my bedroom. I fucking *hated* crying. Shit always left me with a puffy face and a headache.

"Angel, please don't cry. Let me explain," Santo's voice pleaded from the doorway.

I didn't want to face him, but Marco pulled back, making me clutch at him in my panic to not be left alone with Santos right then.

"Taking my shirt off, Paradise. I told you, I'm not going anywhere. This right here..." He took my left hand in his, rubbing the pad of his thumb over the ring that added a minuscule but mighty weight. "This is my promise, where you can see it anytime you need it."

At my nod, he stepped back and tugged his shirt off before wiping at my soggy face and earning a watery laugh in return. Then the shit toed off his shoes and flopped back on my bed with his arms behind his head, leaving me without a barrier between me and the source of my fresh heartbreak.

"Well, I'm waiting." My tone was waspish, but fuck him for making me cry after I'd sworn more than once that I was done with waterworks over Santos DeLuca. Needing more fortification than I could manage on my own, I retreated to sit on the edge of my bed, feeling stronger with Marco at my back. Something Santos didn't miss or care for, according to the narrowed-eye look he directed behind me.

"I never said I didn't want to marry you. I said that I *can't*. It's not safe; you'd be better off with Tony or Vanni or even Marco than me. I'm the muscle, Eden, the shield, if you will. You'll always be in some danger thanks to being associated with us at all. But in the grand scheme of things? I'm the one that's technically replaceable in the organization; the others can give you a stability that I can't promise." I vaguely understood what he meant, but I didn't agree with it.

"You're not fucking replaceable like goddamned batteries, Santos. Just tell me that you don't want to and fucking own up to it already." My heart was hardening by the second, and I didn't even reprimand Marco for lighting up in the house and passing me the lit cigarette with the water glass from my nightstand to ash in. Tony could fuck himself on his rule today.

Santos clenched his fists as he glared at me until he finally spit out his reply. "Vinnie wouldn't give a fuck if you were my wife, Eden. I thought you already understood that from our conversation last week! You'd be expendable right along with me. Tony would be best, but he said you were against it, so that leaves Vanni or Marco. *None* of us would be anything except ecstatic to be your husband, but we all want you safe, and I'm not that option!" His shout was punctuated by what I took to be Marco's grunt of agreement.

I turned to look at him, questions in my head that I was afraid to ask, but he answered them anyway.

"He's right, Edie, but I wasn't going to push you into anything you don't want to do or dissuade you from finally getting what you should have gotten years ago. You and Santos were it, we all knew it, so it doesn't hurt any of us to let you have that now. We'd have made it work, still will if that's what you decide." The last was directed more at Santos than me, and I had a feeling that Santos would be the one at the business end of the shotgun if he refused to comply with my wishes.

I *almost* laughed at the notion of it, but sadness crept in because they were both right. Tony was in the same shoes I'd been in before Santos had spilled the truth. None of us were particularly good at managing words when our emotions were high, which explained Tony's sourpuss attitude on the porch. Juggling all their asses was going to be hard work. At least Marco was somewhat levelheaded.

He got up to crack the window as I smoked and tried to figure out what to do. In the end, I couldn't decide at all.

"Why do I even need to do this? Tony was just pissed that I was baiting him. I think we've established that I'm not going anywhere." At their silence, I glanced from one to the other and dropped my cigarette in the glass to put it out. "What? Did something happen?"

Santos shrugged and rubbed a tattooed hand through his close-cut hair. "It might have been a spur of the moment thing, Eden, but it's not a bad idea at this point. Everyone knows you're important to us, but Vinnie is still willing to use you. It would force his hand on the subject without causing a rift we can't afford right now." He hesitated, looking at Marco before fixing his eyes back on me. "We're done waiting around, baby. Things are only getting worse, and I'll need to do my job soon."

"How are you planning to do that when you're under house arrest?" Then it dawned on me as I handed the glass off to Marco. "Vanni can get around the monitors, can't he?" It wasn't really a question, but I had more important issues than Giovanni's tech skills. "You're going after Rodrigo. When were you going to tell me this?" My voice was strained from all my crying, but on top of it, my throat felt strangled by my fear. *He's going to get himself killed.*

"As soon as he makes his presence known, yes, I am. It would already be done if we knew where he was, but he planned this takeover for a long time and knew what he was doing." His tortured blue eyes met my green ones while I contemplated all the ways their plans could go wrong. Not to mention he was talking about murdering his own father. Could he even do it?

I crossed my arms, hurt and anger warring in me equally. "So what, you think you'd leave me a widow? Or you want to make sure I'm taken care of if you're not around to do it?"

"Both," he gritted out, crossing his arms across his chest, making his t-shirt strain with the move. "He had my house hit yesterday. I'd already moved most of what I didn't want to part with here, but that's a pretty fucking clear sign that I'm dead to him. It's also something we can't ignore without losing face, or we take the chance of more men defecting to his side."

The blood drained from my head fast enough to leave me dizzy. There was a very real possibility I would lose him again. It was a good thing I was already sitting down, or I'd have fallen on my ass. *Will any of us ever get to be happy?*

I excused myself to shower and asked if they minded putting my lunch in the microwave until I could come down to eat it. Seemed I had decisions to make, and not only about who I was going to marry.

eighteen
shivers

Tony

Last Night

I sat next to Santos, watching Eden as Vanni and Marco took turns feeding her bites directly from the cake Marco had ordered. It was some chocolate monstrosity that hadn't been picked up, and Marco had paid who-knew-what to get them to hand it over. But the joy on Eden's face was worth whatever it was. I only wished she'd been that happy as we'd signed the marriage license. Instead, she'd tried to hide the guilt and worry that plagued her when Santos had stepped up as one of the witnesses. I'd wanted to kick his ass when he'd refused, but he'd made his case, and I couldn't exactly argue with it. It was the truth, but my feelings were torn between shame over stealing my best friend's girl and being satisfied that she was officially mine.

When she'd tried to apologize for outright refusing to entertain the idea of marrying me, I'd waved her off. I knew I'd been over the top, didn't mean it hadn't been a kick in the gut, but I understood where she was coming from. I hated that it was bittersweet for her and Santos, though, and I would do everything I could to keep us all together. The idea of packing up and abandoning it all, maybe moving abroad, had crossed my mind more than once. Leave the fucking city to Rodrigo and the Finellis, let them duke it out while we worked on our tans on some beach and enjoyed our lives. The only thing stopping me was the people that would be left behind to deal with the fallout, the ones that had been loyal to the Carlotti Family for decades. Which was why Santos and I had decided that we had to cut the head off of the snake and brutally make an example out of those that had gone against us. It was past time for the end game.

"Hey, jackass! Get over here!" Vanni's shout brought me out of my brooding thoughts to find they had lined up champagne glasses.

Determined to make the best of the night for Eden's sake, I joined the party and even grudgingly laughed at the ridiculous toast he and Marco came up with.

By the time midnight rolled around, we'd moved to the den and polished off several bottles of champagne. Eden was curled up in Santos' lap on one of the sofas while Vanni and Marco played a board game the rest of us had lost interest in. There was some sort of bet involved, but I couldn't be bothered to keep track of what it was this time.

"Hey, angel, are you about ready for bed?" I heard Santos quietly ask a sleepy Eden. At her nod, he levered himself to his feet, with her in his arms.

"Night, lovebirds," Vanni called out without looking up; Marco echoed him, also blowing a kiss like the sappy fuck that he was.

I couldn't begrudge Santos a wedding night after I'd taken his bride, so I resigned myself to going to bed alone. I was going to give them a headstart and clean up some of the mess until I knew they'd be behind closed doors, away from my jealous ass.

Ignoring the comments from the drunken pair, I collected glasses and dishes and took them to the kitchen, leaving it all on the island for housekeeping to deal with. As I drank water and took pain relievers to counteract the headache I knew was coming from the champagne, I gave up trying to stall and headed for my room. Only to find Eden in my bed, a very naked Eden from the lack of clothing covering her back. *Fucking Santos, I can't believe he did this. Or that she went along with it.* But there she was, asleep with her dark hair fanned out over my pillow, too tempting by half. If I got in that bed, there was little chance that I'd keep my hands to myself. I didn't *do* sleepovers, wasn't my thing, and now I had the woman that I'd set my sights on within arm's reach.

"Don't just stand there, Antonio. Get into bed." I turned, heart thumping, as I reached for my gun, the one I wasn't wearing, to glare at Santos.

"I thought you'd left. Did you forget where your room is and put Eden in here by mistake?" It was an inane comment, but I wasn't sure what the fuck was happening, and I didn't care for not being the one in control.

"She's tired and was worried about hurting your feelings. I told her we could all sleep in here, so get in the damn bed, Tony." My closest friend glared at me, daring me to reject my sleeping wife's wishes. *Eden Moretti is my wife.* It hit me then that I was fucking *married.* It hadn't set in yet despite the papers and impromptu party. My wife, in my bed, sealed the deal.

"Right, got it." I swallowed, suddenly nervous but determined not to show it. I wasn't a fucking pansy-assed boy, and I wasn't about to act like one.

Santos raised a scarred brow at me but refrained from commenting, then the bastard stripped down to his boxers and took *my* side of the damn bed. It was closest to the door, so I let it go, figuring his need to be between Eden and anything that could possibly make it to my bedroom was more important than my preference. Besides, I doubted I'd be getting much sleep with Eden between us.

R ight as I started to doze off, Eden shifted, pulling the blankets from me. I'd reached in the dark to take them back from the thief, wholly unused to having to deal with that sort of thing, when she whispered that she had to pee. Apparently, she'd rather climb over me than wake Santos, not that I blamed her; he could be a dick if you startled him while sleeping. I was actually surprised that it hadn't seemed to be an issue, but she'd continued to bunk with him every night without a complaint.

"Shit, sorry," she muttered as I jerked away when her knee landed a bit too close to my junk for comfort. She ended up sprawled across me with her hair in my face, giggling as I tried to spit it out, but fuck, I was drowning in the thick tresses. And trying very hard not to find out if she had anything on. There was a lot of fucking exposed skin anywhere my arms and legs touched her. I deeply regretted wearing a t-shirt to bed.

My patience ran out, and I ended up pushing her back to the middle and rolling off the bed to stand while she got up.

"Bathroom is over there," I helpfully pointed out. In the dark. With a low groan at my redundant comment, I turned on one of the bedside lamps. "There, now you can see." And so could I, and no, there was definitely *not* a stitch of clothing on her. "I'm going to get a drink. You need anything?" I needed to get out of there before my twitching dick made a tent out of my underwear. We hadn't discussed a traditional wedding night, and I didn't feel right assuming she wanted to—although the lack of clothing was leading me to believe that she wouldn't be opposed.

"Water would be good if you don't have the paper cups in your bathroom," she said in a yawn as she padded across the room, not caring a bit that I stared at her ass as she went.

"I do. They're on the inside of the cupboard door. I'll be right back." I did grab a water bottle from the fridge, mostly to kill time until Eden was back in bed, but I also checked on my brother and cousin to see if they were still up.

When I poked my head into the den, I found them both passed out on the oversized sofas, and from the dick drawn on his face in marker, Vanni had crashed first. He was going to be pissed when he woke up. I was still chuckling when I made it back to my bedroom, Eden peering at me in the low-light like I was the nutjob she'd accused me of being earlier. Or maybe that was crackpot, I couldn't remember for sure.

"Must have been a fascinating trip to the kitchen." I had a feeling she wasn't planning on going back to sleep, so I explained as I got into bed after depositing my water on the floor. Didn't want water rings on my table. "Well, Marco warned him he'd better not fall asleep first." She shrugged and snuggled into me after pulling my arm out to rest under her head.

What the fuck is happening? Eden's lack of personal boundaries was throwing me off. She was quick to touch or be close with the others, but in my case, other than the occasional hug, she usually steered clear.

"Eden, I'm not sure I can sleep like this," I ventured, hoping it wouldn't hurt her feelings. Not that I dared to move until she released me.

"You used to call me Edie, too. Or did you forget that?" The change in subject had me forgetting about my trapped arm.

"I did," I agreed, my tone exposing the wariness I felt at her question.

"How come you don't now? The others do." I felt her tip her head up to stare at me when I didn't answer, but I didn't really have one for her.

"Not sure why, but it felt odd when I tried it out

in my head, so I just haven't." I shrugged, not sure how to explain it. "Is there something wrong with me calling you Eden?" I didn't have some pet name for her like Santos or Marco. Damn woman was putting me on the spot, and I didn't have a clue why.

"No reason, really, was just curious." And she fucking tucked her head onto my chest before throwing a leg over my waist. It pressed her hot core against my hip, something I fucking knew she had to be aware of, and acted like she was going back to sleep.

"Alright, you little minx, you're doing that on purpose," I accused, stretching my free arm out to turn off the lamp.

The shaking of her shoulders, accompanied by her breath puffing against my chest, was all the reaction she gave.

"Eden, you are naked, and I'm trying really fucking hard to behave like the gentleman that we both know I'm not." She was going to make me into the batshit crazy person she'd accused me of being with her uncomfortably personal questions that led nowhere, and now *this*.

"I really don't recall asking you to attempt to act like one, Antonio. If you'd rather sleep, tell me now."

Her warning was immediately followed by her hand taking mine and guiding it between her legs. The brief graze from her piercings perked my interest, but she had a different destination in mind, and my dick went from twitching to straight up saluting as she pressed my middle finger into her slick heat, right along with her own.

"Kiss me, Tony," she demanded, tipping her head up to mine while forcing the apex of her cunt against my palm as she ground herself on my hand.

No fucking way could I refuse her. For weeks, I'd been dying to get my hands on her, and I'd felt my chances with her slipping through my fingers earlier in the day. Now she was my fucking wife...and I planned to show her that I could be something other than the hardass that she liked to call me.

Taking charge of the situation, I rolled until she was on her back, hovering over her, only briefly pausing when I remembered Santos was in the bed. But if he was awake, he was doing a damn good job of pretending not to be. "You know I care about you, quite a lot, to be clear, and this isn't only about sex, right?" I was no good at this shit, but I'd try. For her. My wife. *I have a fucking wife.* It was still surreal, but I imagined it was the same for Eden, so I tried not to make a big deal about it.

"I care about you quite a lot, too, Tony, but I'm after the sex at the moment, if you don't mind."

"Fuck no, I don't mind. Try not to wake your boyfriend up when you call my name as you come on my cock." I swallowed her laughing complaint about all of us being possessive heathens before pillaging her mouth with my tongue.

I couldn't get enough of her. Her silky skin, her scent, the way her breath caught in her throat, and her back arched when I sucked on her pert nipples or her faint moans as I curled my fingers just right inside her soaked pussy. It seemed she felt the same as she divested me of my shirt and boxers before wrapping long limbs around me, holding me close as we made out, nipping and sucking at each other's lips and tongues between tangling duels of the latter. My cock throbbed with the need to be inside her, but I didn't want to rush her. Besides, I was quite enjoying the satiny slide of her pussy lips against the underside of my erection. Until I accidentally pushed when she arched, and I pressed halfway into her before realizing I didn't have a condom on or any on this side of the bed. Waking Santos up for a rubber seemed tacky, but I really didn't want to have to get up either. "I need to get a condom," I apologized as I pulled out.

But she didn't let me go far, pushing me down on the bed with a hand to my chest as she leaned over to get into the drawer. I was going to tell her there wasn't anything in there, but the rattle of a bag had me holding my tongue. Only able to see shadows, I regretted shutting the light off, but soon enough, she was joining me back in bed.

"I planned ahead, Mr. Mafia Boss. I even have condoms if you'd like."

"Hell no, not if you're covered with whatever

you just did. One of the perks of having a wife has to be the ability to go bareback," I teased her as she tried and failed to straddle me. I was going to be on top; something about my weight over hers, my body caging hers in, was flat out doing it for me.

"Then get to it, husband," she snarked back.

A moment later, I had one of her legs around my waist and the other over my shoulder. As I pressed my chest to hers and took her lips with mine, I filled her pussy, stretching her on my dick until I'd buried it deep inside. We moved together, her tight walls grasping at me until I couldn't hold on any longer, working a hand between us to thumb her clit until she came clenching around my own pulsing member.

Something loosened in my chest as I fell to the side, releasing her leg and pulling her over to blanket my body. *I fucking loved my wife.* I couldn't find the words just yet, but the last bit of doubt that I'd held onto, the one that said she'd never fully accept me after how I'd treated her, dispersed in the afterglow of my first foray into lovemaking. Fucking would likely be on the agenda most times, but I had to admit, this sweet shit wasn't half bad.

"I have to pee again," Eden mumbled sleepily against my chest.

I didn't want her to move, happy to have her stay there despite my earlier misgivings about personal space. "You can hold it, Eden. You're a big girl."

"Fuck you, asshole," she responded without

much heat. "Pee after sex, dude! No UTIs up in this bitch. Besides, between the gel shit and your spunk and mine, I have a hell of a mess that's going to come back out sooner than later." She slid off of me as Santos finally lost it, laughing at her tirade, proving he had not been sleeping. At least not for all of our activities.

In the dark, I scowled in his general vicinity, hoping he'd not heard any of what I'd had to say. It was bad enough that I'd vocalized my shit to Eden; I didn't need Santos poking me about it later. Not that that was something he'd usually do, but we were all in uncharted territory at this point.

"Hurry up, angel. Get back to bed. I sleep better with you next to me." And wasn't that the fucking truth. I wondered if it would be the same for me, and I looked forward to finding out as a yawn cracked my jaw wide.

nineteen

outrunning karma

Santos

In The Present

Tony looked up at me, pale as fuck, as Marco and Vanni joined us, but he didn't take his eyes off of me as they took their seats in his office. I'd been on my way in when he'd bellowed for his brother, but his attention had been pulled to his phone, and then he'd gone several shades lighter in an instant.

I didn't want him to say it. If he kept his fucking mouth shut, I wouldn't have to hear whatever news he had to deliver. My head shook even as he opened his mouth.

"He has her," Tony stated simply. I knew the 'he' was my father, and the 'her' was Eden. He didn't have to spell it out. As red began to creep into my vision, loss and rage mixing to form something toxic and deadly, Tony tried to forestall the freak-out we both knew was coming. "She's alive, and my father has a meeting with Rodrigo to get her back. We'll bring her home, Santos." But none of it mattered. We both knew she wouldn't be safe, not with *him*. And for sure, not after he discovered she had a new surname. It was only a matter of time before the license was processed, and the rumors began to flow.

Eden

My hands shook as I drank water straight from the showerhead. Part of it was due to hunger after no longer being used to the twisting pains and vacillating blood sugar levels starving caused. My last meal had been late afternoon yesterday, not that I'd been able to eat much. But the other part was the fact that after I'd eventually fallen asleep, I'd been woken up to Rodrigo pinning me down on my stomach before he roughly fucked me from behind while he told me of his plans for today. Afterward, insomnia had struck, joining the sick feeling his words and touch had left behind.

With my hands tied to the post of the headboard, I was unable to get up. Regardless, I was afraid to move after he'd dared me to wipe his seed away. So I laid there, tears flowing silently down my cheeks, soaking the pillow as my promise to the guys played through my head on repeat.

Eventually, I got my crying under control, but that didn't change the fact that I was trapped with a sadistic, rapist asshole, only able to watch as the time ticked by, one red number on the digital alarm clock at a time. Finally, the alarm clicked on, a harsh buzzing waking Rodrigo from his snoring slumber. He got up with a groan, stretching as he went to take a piss. The stream hitting the water, loud in the otherwise silent room, prompted my bladder to let it be known that it too needed to relieve itself. But first, I had to suffer through Rodrigo coming back, stroking his morning wood before he climbed between my legs to rut into me again. I'd turned my head, trying to ignore that it was *him* on me, when he slapped my face and made me watch as he grunted his way to completion.

He'd left me there, dripping with his cum, while he showered, then untied me and told me to do the same.

I did my best to scrub him from my body, desperately hoping that he hadn't gotten me pregnant and trying to figure out how to warn the guys without access to a phone.

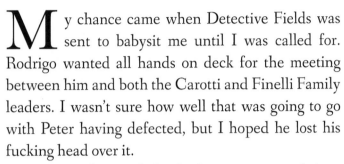

My chance came when Detective Fields was sent to babysit me until I was called for. Rodrigo wanted all hands on deck for the meeting between him and both the Carotti and Finelli Family leaders. I wasn't sure how well that was going to go with Peter having defected, but I hoped he lost his fucking head over it.

I stepped out of the bathroom, wrapped in a towel, to find Fields waiting for me.

"What the fuck do you want? Come to take your poke at the pie?" I snarled at him, wanting to do him some serious bodily harm.

He held out a piece of black fabric, guilt-ridden but silent until I stalked across the floor and jerked it from his hand. Not caring that he was in the room, I dropped the towel and pulled the tube-dress over my head. Of course, there wasn't any fucking underwear, but at least my boots were salvageable.

"So, are you going to explain or just hide your face like a pearl-clutching twat when confronted with a pair of boobs?" I didn't wait for his reply, going in search of something to brush my hair. Unless I could get to the dressing room or have someone bring cosmetics up, there wasn't much I could do with my face or the bruises and road rash dotting my exposed skin. Searching the bathroom had only turned up a bunch of Danny's shit dumped into boxes, but deodorant was deodorant to me—better than smelling like Rodrigo.

Having done what I could, I went back out to stare at the detective until he found his tongue.

"I'm sorry, Eden. This is not what I meant to happen. Here, call your men. I've had a hell of a time keeping them out of police custody. I can only radio in so many false reports before I'll be sitting next to them in a cell." He sounded sincere enough, and he was holding a phone out, but I worried that it was a trap.

Danny hadn't kept surveillance in his rooms. Out in the hall, yes, but not anywhere he spent a lot of private time. Since Fields was being seemingly candid, I could only hope that Rodrigo hadn't changed the practice—not that they really had anything left to threaten me with if they caught me. The room was windowless, so I was essentially stuck unless I could get past my guard, which further reinforced my thinking that it was safe enough to speak plainly. I also didn't think we'd been left a way out. Rodrigo wasn't the type to leave things to chance. I doubted we'd make it very far even if I could convince Fields to get me out of there.

"What are you getting out of this, Detective? You have to admit, you've played all the sides beautifully, or at least competently enough since you're still in the game and free to move about." I took the phone he'd offered, but I held on to it until he answered me.

"Let's just say I have some personal beef with the parties involved and leave it at that, please," he evaded before clamming up again.

Not wanting to waste any more time, I took the cell into the bathroom, turned on the water in the sink and shower, and locked the door. I didn't know how well it would cover my voice or if the call would be recorded, but it was the best I could do under the circumstances.

Then I had the dilemma of who to call. Vinnie was out as far as I was concerned, likely already on his way to the meeting anyway, and I needed the guys to be at home, where they were safe. I finally settled on calling Marco, the most level-headed of the four.

It rang for so long that I worried he wouldn't answer, and when his voice came on the line, it wasn't his voicemail.

"Why the fuck are you calling me, Fields?" *Well, he's the most level-headed of the four, not in general.*

"I don't have long, and I need you to listen."

"Edie? Oh, thank fuck, he got you out. Are you okay? Where are you? We'll meet you." The relief in his voice hurt my heart, knowing that I had to tell him that I wasn't free. Not yet. But the others must have been with him as their voices came through the speaker in spurts and starts until Santos won the argument.

"Angel, baby, tell us where you are," he demanded, with Marco bitching at him that he'd just fucking asked that while Tony cursed at someone for not using a turn signal.

"Why are you out of the house?! Get home *now*, Santos!" I did my best to keep my voice down, but I was panicked. When Fields had talked about keeping them out of jail, I'd assumed they'd gone home, where they *really* needed to be. Fucking should have known that they wouldn't stay put, not that I could blame them. What a goddamned clusterfuck.

"We're coming to get you, Eden. Don't fuck around! Tell me if you're hurt and where to pick you up." He was equally as pissed, but they couldn't get to me, and I couldn't leave even if they did.

"I'm in Danny's old room at Cherry Baby, and I'm fine," I told him, trying to get him to shut up. I couldn't tell him what had happened. He had me on speaker now, so their collective curses came through loud and clear, but I ignored them in favor of getting my warning out. "You *cannot* come here. Rodrigo has plans, Santos. If you're not at home when the police conduct a supposedly random check, you're going straight back to jail. You know none of you will come back out if that happens. You can't bust me out of here; they're waiting on it... I'm honestly not sure if

Vinnie will get back out, either," I added, reluctant to tell them the full extent of it. "You show up here, and he for sure won't. Your father, he doesn't care anymore, Santos. He's only doing any of this to toy with us all, to flex his power and to punish those that went against him. Namely, you and me, and to an extent, Vinnie and the guys."

Calmer now, but with trepidation lacing his voice, he asked, "Eden, how do you know all of this, and why can't you leave with Fields? He's there with you, is he not?"

I didn't want to answer him, but he'd find out eventually. "He has all of Danny's insurance, Santos." Tony's voice came through above the others, bitching about Danny lying to him. *Of fucking course, Danny lied. He liked his head attached, not that it helped him in the end.* But that wasn't important at the moment; we couldn't change the past.

"It's not only Tony and Vanni who will go down... I'm in them too, and I doubt the statute of limitations is up on most of it. I-I know where the hard copies are, and I can get to them, but I can't do anything about what he's uploaded to whatever cloud network thing he's made. I don't know what it is exactly, and my knowledge on technology is seriously limited to basic shit like phones and what I learned in school," I admitted, too worried to feel more than marginally embarrassed by my lack of skills. "As for the rest, yes, Fields is here. He brought me his phone, but he can't get me out, and Rodrigo was happy to tell me what he'd do if you didn't stay out of it. He has plans, real ones, and it would garner him public support to turn his own son over." It wasn't the whole story, but it was the truth, and it was all that I needed them to know for now.

"This isn't your fight. We can't leave you there. *I* can't leave you there. Please don't ask me to," Santos begged, voice strained with emotion.

My own was full of pity—for him, me, for all of us. "This has been my fight since I was unlucky enough to have been born to the parents I was. It's been my fight since I walked into your house and fell in love with you. And it's most certainly been my fight since we did what teenagers do—seventeen, in lust, and ready to dip our toes into the adult world, we made the choices that forged our paths. Right or wrong, this is where it's led. I can't change that, Santos, and neither can you. Whatever I did or didn't do in a past life has thrown me back into the shit over and over. Figure out how to erase the evidence, and I'll *gladly* do my best to get out of here. As it stands, they're prepared for us to try to make it out of the city. All I can hope for now is that Vinnie can make a deal." I figured it was unlikely that Rodrigo would let me go, but a girl could hope.

"I won't let you go, angel, never again." Santos was adamant, but so was I.

"I'm sorry, baby, but you have to...at least for

today." A knock came at the door, followed by Fields calling my name. I cracked it, hiding the phone against my side while he told me I had only a few minutes before we had to leave. I shut the door in his face and brought the phone up again. "I have to go. They're calling me in. Just promise me you'll go back to the house for now. You can leave later, when it's safer. Believe me, I don't want to fucking be here any more than you want me here. And Tony, I'm sorry I argued with you. I should have let you handle it."

"We'll talk about it when you're home. I'm turning around for now, counting on my father to bring you home, but fair warning, if he doesn't show up, we'll be coming for you.

The meeting was happening in the same room as before, sans dancers this time. The place looked odd with the dark stages, usually only something that happened after hours, not when the place was packed with armed men. Peter joined me on the opposite side from Fields right before we made it through the crowd and to the table where Rodrigo held court. The detective had to tighten his hold on my elbow as I stumbled, trying to keep from touching the man that thought he shared ownership of me.

A dark chuckle preceded his promise. "I'll be

seeing you after this is over." I didn't bother to respond as he took his seat, but I did feel some relief that they hadn't found out I'd married Tony yet. I didn't think that would do me any favors today, not when Rodrigo was playing fast and loose with any of the unspoken rules the Families generally upheld.

Fields delivered me to Rodrigo's side, then took up a guard position a bit behind and to the side of me while the bane of my existence rested his hand on my ass in full view of everyone. Like I was his whore...and I supposed I was. I gripped my wrist with my other hand, rubbing my birthmark for comfort while I stood in a den of snakes without one person I could truly trust to have my back. That proved true as Vinnie's eyes briefly met mine, a hint of guilt quickly buried under a hard stare, before he ignored me in favor of speaking to Peter.

"After speaking with him this morning, I was under the impression that Edward would be attending today?"

Peter rested his elbows on the table and fixed his attention on Vinnie. "Dad can't make it today. He had an accident on the way in, so I'm the new head of the Finellis. It'll be me you'll be dealing with now. Honestly, I'm surprised Antonio hasn't arranged the same for you, old man, such a shame when things like that could be prevented." The sadness he displayed was blatantly false, but Vinnie's eyes widened just enough to let me, and everyone else, know that the death of his rival had rattled him. My stomach sank further as I realized Vinnie didn't have as much control of the situation as I'd hoped he would. *Why the fuck did he even show up?*

"My condolences, Peter," Rodrigo offered, breaking the silence when the crush of men shifted restlessly. Then he dropped the bombshell I was already aware of. "But I'll extend my offer of partnership to you, just as I did Edward."

"I think we can work well together, DeLuca, but why don't you finish this before we get into the details?"

It was all a farce, set up to play Vinnie and take the power from the Carlotti Family. I was just the icing on the cake; there was little doubt in my mind that all of this would have happened with or without my presence, but it was another power-play aimed at bringing the Carlottis down a peg of four.

Vinnie, out of patience for the bullshit they were dealing, demanded to get down to it. "And what is it that you're hoping to get out of this, Rodrigo? You were a valued member of my organization until you violated our rules—multiple times. Instead of choosing to stay and face your punishment like a man, you stole from me and ran away. You've caused havoc all over the city, had my *son* violated, and now you want to, what, take the spot of the man you murdered?"

The occupants of the room shifted again, but

they calmed when Rodrigo held up a hand, and I had to wonder how many of them were actually there for Vinnie.

"I'm taking over the neutral zone, and I want equal respect from both the Carlotti and Finelli factions. I also control the majority of the law enforcement for the county and will be running for mayor in the next election. At this point, your conciliation is a formality," Rodrigo declared, smug in his confidence. "And I don't mean this will continue to be the territory of no-man's land; it's going to be the hub for everything else. You and Edward were short-sighted in leaving such a gap that could be utilized against you. Now, I believe we have terms to set...or I can dispose of you and deal with your heirs after. It's your choice, Vincenzo."

Not so calm in the face of his comeuppance, Vinnie irately snapped at Rodrigo, "Why don't you enlighten me since you've decided how this is going to go, DeLuca? You're aware I came to broker a truce and retrieve Miss Moretti."

"Ah, yes, your repetitious use of Eden here got on my nerves, so I put a stop to it. I assumed she wasn't important enough for you to bother with after you so carelessly left her unprotected."

I hoped like hell he was talking shit, and Vinnie hadn't actually pulled my detail, not that I wanted them dead, but I'd be after Vinnie's head as well as Rodrigo's if it were true.

"No one said you had to stalk the woman. Besides, it looks as if she's suffered enough at the hands of your men as is," he accused, eyeing my bruises with distaste. At least, I hoped it was the state of my skin and not me in general. I just didn't know anymore. "If you don't mind, my boys are rather fond of her, and I'd like to return her to them."

Rodrigo grinned and squeezed my ass while I gritted my teeth and pretended it wasn't happening. "Oh, this wasn't all their doing, gotta teach a girl her place, you know, but since you brought them up, let's discuss your boys and their current predicament. Right about now, I'd imagine they'll either be home, complying with their random home visit, or there's a manhunt underway." He ignored Vinnie's curse and pale complexion and kept on. "You can agree here and now to fall in line with any directive I see fit on the running of this syndicate and the city, and they can have their freedom, or... I'm sure you can fill in the rest." His shrug indicated he didn't care either way, but his hand had tensed on my backside, and I had to wonder if Vinnie had picked off enough of Rodrigo's men to make the other man unsure of the outcome if it came down to an all-out war in the streets.

"And what about your own son, DeLuca? He's part of Antonio's crew; are you going to make his charges go away as well?" I was surprised he'd even asked, but maybe he didn't want to face his sons if he threw Santos to the wolves.

"My son is dead to me, Vincenzo. I'm thinking about starting over before I'm too old to properly groom my new heir." My eyes slid closed when he pulled me close and curled his palm over my abdomen, but I'd caught enough of Vinnie's expression to know he pitied me.

Silence reigned at the table, and I hoped I was the only one that noticed Fields' sharply indrawn breath at the not-so-subtle announcement. I found my own composure and opened my eyes to find Vinnie staring at the table, presumably weighing his options and gathering his thoughts.

"So, the charges will be dropped, and the witness will disappear? Or take the fall? And as long as the Carlotti Family operates under your umbrella, operations return to normal?" he finally asked, speaking carefully and concisely. Rodrigo nodded, and Vinnie's gaze quickly flicked to me then back to Rodrigo before he made his offer. "Then you'll accept *her* as a token of cooperation between us?"

What the actual fuck?! My mouth was about to run away with itself, consequences be damned, when Rodrigo shocked the shit out of me.

"You're going to hand her over, just like that?" he asked incredulously. "What happened to your high and mighty views on my treatment of her before? Seems you're selling out, old man." Vinnie bristled at

Rodrigo's taunt, then composed himself and shrugged.

"It was about taking care of our own, those under the protections offered by the Family, and following through on our promises. A matter of honor, if you will. You know how it goes. We don't shirk our obligations, but once the loyalties have traded hands," he shrugged and spread his hands, "it's no longer Carlotti business." Vinnie refused to meet my glare, and even Fields stepped closer as if sensing I was two seconds from launching myself across the table.

But my mind was spinning out, and my legs felt too weak to do anything but keep upright, my hands and feet tingling in response to the panic and betrayal coursing through my body. *The fuck really sold me out.* He'd just traded me away, like fucking chattel, not caring what would happen to me. Dread continued to pool in my gut like acid. I could handle it while I knew it was temporary, I could handle it while he exacted his pound of flesh from me for his son for turning against him, but to be at Rodrigo's mercy for the rest of whatever time I had left to live? No, I couldn't do it. I *wouldn't* do it. I'd promised myself not to go back to that life, and I'd just been launched right back into it.

"So be it," Rodrigo replied, loosening his hold on me. "Peter, be a pal and take our new acquisition to wait for me in my office?"

I stiffened, contemplating fighting, as Peter got

up from his seat to collect me, Jasper in tow. When Peter gripped my elbow and gestured for Fields to step back, I turned to follow, flipping Vinnie off as I went. His expression remained hard and unfeeling, but Rodrigo and Peter's muffled laughter said they found it amusing. Again, I imagined smacking them a time or two, but I knew it wouldn't do more than injure any pride I might have left, so I followed like the good little whore they claimed I was.

twenty

scars

Vanni

As soon as the gate closed behind the last officer, I had men checking for anything left behind. Thanks to Eden's warning, we'd been able to make it back on the property through one of the hidden entrances before the police had made it here. We were sweaty as fuck and out of breath from having to make it on foot, so, to avoid having to explain, and to deter them from going in the house, we'd taken up stations around the obstacle course set up outside.

Unable to prove we hadn't been home, exercising the entire time, they'd grudgingly left us in peace. I didn't particularly care if they were pissed or not; my mind was on something, some*one* far more important. Turning around instead of storming the club to get her out hadn't sat well with any of us, and I was itching to remedy the situation. I just needed an opportunity to get at Rodrigo's system, and he wouldn't have jack shit left to hold over any of our heads. In the meantime, I supervised the removal of several surveillance devices then watched the security system in Tony's office, waiting for my father to show up, hopefully with Eden in tow.

T he call came before the cavalcade made an appearance at the gate. Details were withheld, but Eden had *not* returned, and my brother, always needing to be in control, lost his shit and trashed his office.

Santos hadn't seemed the least bit surprised, nor had Marco for that matter, but Tony had been banking on our father bringing her home. I didn't think he'd have actually left her there, cops be damned, if he'd thought there would have been any other outcome. Our enforcer was the one to snap Tony out of his fit, not physically, but by announcing he was going to wait in our father's office and slamming out of the room. There was no doubt that *that* meeting wouldn't go well, so we all quickly followed him. The argument that ensued was not one I'd have ever guessed would take place, not with Tony involved anyway.

"Show some respect, Antonio. I didn't raise you to behave in this manner!"

"You said you'd take care of it. Leaving her behind wasn't part of the deal! I won't leave her with that man, and I don't care who has a fucking problem with it," Tony shouted at our father.

"I kept my word. It's been handled, the charges will be dropped, and you will all be released from house arrest. Compromises were reached. It's not uncommon to settle disputes by joining one of our own with the other party—"

"What the fuck are you talking about, Vinnie? Did you give Eden to my father?" Santos was dead calm, but even my father flinched at the promise of death in his eyes.

"He declared you're dead to him, so I would rethink that title. Miss Moretti did her duty, although it's not in the traditional sense." He muttered the last part as if unhappy about that point, but forged on with a dismissive wave of his hand. "I'm certain once Rodrigo has secured his...future, he'll release her if she wishes it."

I had to admit my father was delusional. Obviously, he didn't want to spell out what the terms were, and I'd come to the conclusion that he'd had his ass handed to him at that meeting.

But Tony, eyes blazing and fists clenched in his fury, informed him of how badly he'd fucked up. "You traded my *wife* to be raped and likely murdered?! You're no longer fit to run this Family. It's past time you joined our mother," he gestured at me, "in her travels."

Having no interest in backing down, our father attempted to take control of the room. "Your *wife?!* Are you insane, Antonio? The girl is nice enough, but she's also trash and wholly unsuitable for you. If DeLuca wants her, who better to infiltrate his operation? It would be stupid to pass up the opportunity."

"I cannot believe you used her like that! My own father! It wasn't your call," Tony retorted, looking like he was about to start in on tearing this room up as well.

"And I cannot believe you share your live-in whore, but here we are," my father shot back with a wave of his hand. Marco darted in front of Santos as I grabbed Tony, my father continuing to dig his hole deeper as far as I was concerned. "It's time you all stopped with whatever the nature of your relationship is anyhow. I would have accepted her with Santos, but how could *you* marry her? And behind my back? You'll have it annulled immediately!" he demanded. "Even your mother did what was required of her to broker peace! How do you think Edward and I came to a truce in the first place? We'd have all killed each other off long before now, and I'm not talking about the little skirmishes your generation has continuously engaged in, but complete annihilation. And you're correct. I'm more than ready to turn all of this over, but I refuse to see it destroyed for a whore!" He silenced everyone as he went off, revealing things that had only been a vague rumor while continuing to insult Eden, and it brought my temper to its breaking point.

"That *whore* is your daughter-in-law," I seethed at the man I'd always looked up to. "And if Tony hadn't married her, *I* would have. We *all* would have. I understand that you wanted to protect us, and maybe you did it the best way you knew how, but cutting us out has caused more trouble than it's solved. Either we work together, and you tell us what you've got in the works, or you catch a plane tonight, and we'll let you know when it's over. You talk about respect, yet you won't give us any of our own. That's not how this family operates, Father." My tirade had a calming effect I hadn't planned on. I wasn't sure if he was shocked that I had called him on his bullshit, or if he realized he'd really fucked up with Eden and that he was about to lose his sons over it, but he shut up and listened. When I finished, still straight-up irate with him, my father nodded his head and pulled out a folder, showing us what he'd been up to with Eden on all of those outings. I knew he loved and wanted to protect us, doing it the only way he knew how, but he was going to have to learn to accept Eden and realize she was off-limits, period.

Eden

I limped into Rodrigo's office on one heel after Jasper had decided to walk too closely behind me. When he'd misstepped, on purpose or not, I wasn't sure, his boot had kicked my foot sideways, snapping the stiletto off and twisting my ankle in the process. My mind had been on all the ways I'd like to castrate Rodrigo and beat the shit out of Vinnie for selling me out, so I was lucky that was all that had happened due to my inattention.

I made it to the couch before I plopped down and got both boots off so I could examine the damage. My injured ankle was already showing signs of purple bruising, and I knew the swelling wouldn't be far behind. *So much for running out of here if the opportunity presents itself.* Not that I'd let a sprained ankle stop me if it meant my freedom.

"Can I get some ice to put on this?" I asked as I

gingerly propped it on the arm of the couch while trying not to flash my goods at the room.

"What do I look like, your bitch? Get it yourself."

"Jasper, you caused it. Go get the fucking ice, and I'll forget that you were going to let her wander off on her own, fucking idiot." Peter muttered the last part under his breath as his cousin left the room before pointing at me. "Don't think that's going to get you out of anything. DeLuca wants you on stage tonight."

I didn't bother to answer, hoping he'd ignore me and leave me to my inner turmoil that was far more painful than my ankle. My wish was granted as he pilfered one of the cigars from the humidor and lit up, but it *almost* had me asking for one... I wanted a cigarette something fierce. I ignored the urge, though, as well as the one that wanted something stronger than nicotine despite my desire to check out from reality. I needed to have my wits about me if I planned on getting out of this mess.

Jasper came back, bag of ice in hand, and glared down at me as he slapped it onto my ankle. "There you go, princess. I'll collect my payment later."

I gritted my teeth against the wince that wanted to surface, but he must have wanted a reaction, or maybe an answer, because he reached down and pressed the ice into the injury. "Get the fuck off!" I snapped at him, kicking his hand away with my good foot. I knew I shouldn't have reacted, shouldn't have engaged, but my anger had boiled over. Paired with my throbbing joint, I lost my temper.

But Jasper had shown his true colors that night months ago in this very club, and he wasn't about to stand for it. "Oh, *I'll* be getting off, and you'll be learning your place, Angel," he hissed at me, yanking me off of the couch to thump onto the floor, adding to my numerous bruises, I was sure.

I cursed at him and pulled against his hold as he dragged me across the floor, ruching my dress halfway up my hips before he stopped.

"What the hell, Jasper? Get your own, you lazy fuck. Leave the whore alone— Goddamnit, what did I say?!" Peter yelled.

It was accompanied by my bloodcurdling scream as Jasper ground the cherry of the cigar against the sole of my foot, scattering bits of hot ash in searing pinpricks of pain across my thighs and abdomen. Though nothing could top the agony of my foot when he let up, pulling the skin with him, only to do it again.

By then, Peter had rounded the desk and stepped over my torso to physically remove his sadistic cousin from me. "Get the fuck out! I'll deal with you later. I have to figure out how to clean up your fucking mess *again*. Don't come whining to me if DeLuca demands reparations. He said she was free to use, not that we could fuck her up!"

"You're a bootlicker, Peter. You think joining

with him is going to be any better than the Carlottis he used to work for? If anything, he'll turn on you, too, and you're too fucking *weak* to do anything about it. You killed your own father, yet you want to reprimand me for putting a whore in her place? Fuck you, I'm out."

The door slammed, leaving me and Peter alone. The man wasn't so self-assured anymore by the way he was raking his hand through his hair and pacing the floor, stealing glances at me while I straightened my dress and whimpered each time the skin on my foot flexed. *I need more ice.* Not that I thought I'd get any at this point. That was about the only thought I had while I inspected the damage through the tears I couldn't hold back. I did my best to keep what I *did* have on the burns after I crawled to where it had fallen and seriously rethought my previous position on the subject of narcotics.

twenty-one

angry too

Fields

"Thanks, Doc. If you don't mind, keep that knowledge between us for now, yeah? I'm having a hard enough time keeping my head on my shoulders between all the players."

"If they directly ask me, I won't lie for you, Detective, but that girl never deserved to be used like this. Vincenzo is a lifelong friend, but he is ruthless when it comes down to it. If you fail to satisfactorily resolve the situation, you'll find that I can be as well." With that parting warning, the doctor rolled his window up and pulled away, leaving me to stow my contraband away.

I blew out a breath as I shut off my car, then got out and rounded the back to get into the trunk. The guys had come through, and I had a duffel bag full of blow and pills to present to my new 'boss.' It was a lucky break that Doc had been available and accommodating, and that Eden's men hadn't caught wind of anything yet. They'd have been hell to keep put if they had, and they were bad enough already.

The bouncer at the entrance gave me the side-eye before ushering me through, though the one guarding Rodrigo's office wasn't so easy to get past.

"Leave it here. I'll take it in when he isn't busy," the burly man directed, indicating a spot near him on the floor.

I shook my head and got a better grip on the strap, not about to be parted from my ticket in, and hopefully, to Eden. "No can do. I have urgent news, and the boss told me all seizures were to be brought directly to him until he deems otherwise. You can let him know I'm here, or I can announce myself. Either way, my information is time-sensitive" The man had to be a neanderthal the way he just stared. "Do you need a fucking vocabulary lesson, or do you just need it dumbed down to understand? Mr. DeLuca's orders, asshole." I enunciated each word, speaking slowly as if the idiot couldn't comprehend basic English. And fuck, maybe he couldn't, because he looked about ready to charge like a bull at a red flag.

Rodrigo must have been keeping an eye on his video feeds since the door swung open, revealing a topless woman in a g-string and high-heels. She held it open while Rodrigo snapped at the guard to stand down.

I stepped past him with a smirk, then nodded at the woman who peered at me through a curtain of auburn curls with haunted blue eyes. The urge to help her was immediate, but I had to shove it down deep lest I fuck up my mission. If I succeeded, she'd be free to leave anyway.

"Detective, why are you gracing me with your presence already? Did I forget summoning you?" The haughty prick was quickly turning into a megalomaniac, his cruelty matching his own overblown imaginings of grandeur.

Unfortunately, I still had to play along. But that was easier said than done after I caught sight of Eden on the couch, shivering and moaning in her sleep, still in the same dress from earlier in the day. "What's wrong with her?" I dared to ask.

Rodrigo waved a hand, disgust twisting his face as he absentmindedly explained without taking his eyes from his screen.

"Jasper Finelli. He tripped her or some shit and then took offense to getting her ice. She kicked him, so he burned her. With one of my cigars, I might add...the prick. Anyway, this one is here to get her in shape to go on stage in a few hours." As if realizing he was rambling, he looked up at me with tired eyes, the lines in his face more pronounced than usual, showing his age. "Why are you here again?"

Not wanting to push my luck by setting the bag in the chair, I pulled out a handful of the goods. "Seizure. You said you wanted them delivered immediately. I had to get them out now anyway. Higher-ups just got wind that IA is coming, so they've called in everyone to make sure their noses are clean. You'll be down some hands tonight, and probably for a bit more than that."

Those tired eyes lit with a rage to rival Santos', and I imagined this was where he'd inherited his temper from. "You should have led with that, Detective, rather than the rest of the bullshit. You've not been privy to everything since there was little need, but I have to have the forces' support, or we're going to have problems."

"Hey," I held out my hands, "just the messenger here. We both know I don't have any say, especially after barely being reinstated."

He pondered my sincerity, making me sweat when he gave me the side-eye, but eventually, his shoulders relaxed as he nodded. "Fine, take that and lock it in my bedroom. I'll have it sorted through later. Got too many *employees* that would off their grandmother for that bag." When I hesitated, he snapped at me. "What are you waiting for? Go on."

"Do you want me to take her with me? So she can

sort herself out? Your girl there looks like she can barely lift herself." It was a gamble, but I needed Eden out of the vicinity so she couldn't be blamed for what was about to happen.

Rodrigo chuckled, but it wasn't a pleasant sound. "She must have given you better head than she did me if you're after a repeat. Or is your loyalty to her, and not me, Detective?" I shook my head, about to deny the accusation, but he cut me off. "You shouldn't show your hand and expose your weaknesses so easily. This time, it works in your favor, or mine rather. Gives me another piece of insurance to keep you in line. Go on, take her out of here but keep your dick to yourself." He tossed a set of keys at the woman, trying to make herself part of the decor. She caught them, just barely, and held them away from her like they might bite her. "Let them in, then bring them back. I have need of your assistance."

Neither she nor I argued with the directive. I scooped Eden up while the woman again held the door for me before hurrying ahead to open the bedroom. I blocked her and kicked the door shut, daring her to leave before I'd sat Eden down.

"Give me a sec, Eden," I said as she stared at me with confusion and pain in her eyes. "I need to take care of something." Leaving her side, I pulled the other woman into the bathroom. "Do you want out of here? Permanently?" At her rapid nodding, I reached into the inner pocket of my jacket and pulled out the thumb drive to show her. "You plug this into DeLuca's laptop, do what you have to to get out of there, then head out back. Two blocks over, you'll find my partners. There's a duffel bag full of cash and train tickets waiting for you. Don't arouse suspicion. Just do your thing and run, got it?"

"How do I know you're not lying to me? And what if I can't get to it?" she asked warily.

"You don't, but if you refuse to do this, I'll tell him you smuggled the USB in here. Who's he going to believe? And don't worry about an opportunity. I have that covered. You want that money, or do you want to be a traitor? Your call."

With shaking fingers and a glare that quickly shriveled under my uncompromising stare, she took the USB and slipped it under the instep of her high-heel. There weren't really too many other places to hide it, and I was glad she hadn't tried.

"Thank you..."

"Elodie," she reluctantly gave up when I twirled my finger impatiently. I had a hunch that it was her real name and not some stage moniker.

"Thank you, Elodie. Tell them Fields sent you. They'll know if it's working by the time you reach them, and if it is, they'll hand you the cash. Maybe grab something to wear on your way out, yeah?" She nodded and hurried off, leaving me to send a message to Vanni to hit the fire alarm sensors in a few minutes. Hopefully, Rodrigo wouldn't kick the woman out of his office while he went to handle the alarm.

With that done, I turned my attention to Eden and her injuries. Her men were going to string me up with my own intestines for those alone, not to mention what would happen if Rodrigo had already gotten her pregnant...

I'd managed to get some food into Eden as well as some elephant-strength pain killers she'd found in the box of Danny's old shit. After helping her shower, getting cussed at for being a prude when I kept my eyes closed as much as possible, I carried her to the dressing room. Under her direction, I got her foot and ankle taken care of and covered it all up with the schoolgirl's uniform she'd be taking the stage in. I didn't know how the fuck she could walk, let alone stand in the heels she had on, but after she popped a third pill like a Chiclet, I started to get an idea.

"Give 'em here, Eden," I demanded, hand out and no-nonsense expression in place.

"Fuck you, I'm in pain," she retorted, tucking the remaining pills into her bra before somewhat reassuring me. "My tolerance isn't as high as it used to be, but I won't take more unless I can't get off my feet soon."

"Fine, but you're giving up whatever you have when we're through here," I replied, not about to give in. They weren't her drug of choice, but I didn't think she'd be all that picky if she really wanted to backslide.

All I got was an eye roll and a smartass reply. "Yes, Dad, I'll behave." My wince had the ghost of a smile floating around her lips. "Seriously, Detective, you're a fucking prude. But please tell me it worked?" I quickly looked around, worried she might have been overheard.

"Shh, not discussing this now, but yes." I shouldn't have been surprised she'd heard me and the woman, Elodie, in the bathroom. Eden was quite good at using any angle to her advantage if she was at all able to. The fire alarm had gone off while I helped her clean up, so Vanni was probably wiping Rodrigo's system as we spoke.

"Good. Alright, help me out there. The less time on my feet, the better. Gonna be a pole-hanging night," she snickered, eyes bright from the narcotics under all the heavy makeup.

I groaned at her morbid sense of humor but did as she requested, running into a snag with the announcer.

"What the fuck is wrong with my stage name?"

she bitched when she was told she had to pick some-thing else.

"Boss' orders, Angel. Pick something else."

"Fine," she said with a sly smile that worried me. Not that I was sure what trouble she could cause with a fucking name. "Paradise. And play the Guns n' Roses song to match, please." He eyed her before shrugging and marking it down. He knew something was up as well as I did, but neither of us had a clue, and hopefully, neither would Rodrigo.

"I'm going to leave you here if you're good," I said, just out of sight on the side of the stage.

"Yep, you do your thing, Fields, and I'll do mine." With a wink, she composed herself and waited on her cue. If I didn't know better, I'd have never guessed that she was hurt.

I came up next to Rodrigo, who was working the room, trying to keep everything as it should be without the cops that moonlighted as extra guards for him.

"How's it going, boss?" I asked, wanting to keep him close to me and away from Eden. Even on the stage, I didn't dare trust that she was safe from him.

"You have a peculiar habit of turning up and being conveniently seen when you would otherwise need an alibi, Detective." Before he could expand on whatever accusation he was about to lay at my feet, the decades-old, familiar beat and guitar chords of *Paradise City* filtered through the open room. "We have an old friend back in action tonight, gentlemen! She might look like an innocent angel, but tonight, we welcome Paradise!"

Eden strutted onto the stage, suggestively sucking on a cherry red lollipop amid catcalls as the customers realized it was her. Rodrigo, on the other hand, was already moving through the crowd toward the stage, fury emanating from him.

"She found a way around it anyway, fucking bitch. She's *mine* now, not *his!*"

I could only guess that he knew what the new name meant and that it had to do with his estranged son since he was headed exactly where I *didn't* want him—straight for Eden. My thumbs flew across the screen as I shot off a text telling the Carlottis to hurry the fuck up. An answering text came in, simply saying 'Here' before I pocketed my phone and chased after Rodrigo.

Of course, the fuckers came in and caused a stampede when they fired shots into the ceiling. Customers and employees alike fled for the exits that didn't host the gunmen, not that it did a whole lot of good. More men flowed in from the recesses of the club, but at least they ushered the dancers and waitresses out before putting down anyone else that even thought about putting up a fight.

I was still on my mission to get to Eden without getting shot, staying to the edges of the room and holding up my hands while yelling I was with Tony.

"I'm trying to get to Eden. She's on the stage!" The man became helpful then, clearing a path much faster than I had been able to. Some days, being a cop was not in my favor, especially around this crowd.

As the club emptied of patrons, I caught a glimpse of Eden's men ruthlessly tearing through their enemies, leaving a trail of bodies behind them to bleed out on the floor. They'd catch up soon, so I'd better have Eden safe and secured, or they just might add me to the body count. I tried to ignore those who were caught in the crossfire, knowing that they had to have been aware of the risks before they chose to show up.

"Get the fuck off of me, you piece of shit! You're *done,* asshole!" Eden's voice came from the side of the stage, but the lack of visuals made it so I could only imagine what was going on out of sight.

I rounded the corner, stopping dead when the man that had been clearing my way dropped, clutching his thigh and cursing when he couldn't return fire. Rodrigo had one arm around Eden, the other pointing the gun at her head. *At least he's alive,* I thought as I stepped over him, palms up.

"Don't hurt her, DeLuca. Just let me have her," I pleaded despite the futility of it.

"Hurt her? Why the hell would I do that? The whore is my ticket out of here," he replied, brows arched, looking at me like *I* was the fucking idiot. He had to know he wouldn't make it out of here, but he kept talking like he would. "I should have known you weren't to be trusted. What's your plan? Grab the girl and keep her for yourself? I promise, her pussy isn't worth it."

"You're the one assuming I'm not on your side. I don't want to see her hurt; there's a difference." I was trying to buy time, but I wasn't sure what the fuck I would be able to do. Then the Carlotti men coming around the corner shot any chance I might have had all to shit.

They drew up behind me, hurling threats at Rodrigo while Eden stood there, gun to her head and...not fucking seeming concerned in the least. *Did she take more pills?* But her wink and pointed glance down had my eyes widening. She'd picked up a lighter somewhere and was surreptitiously trying to light it. I looked away from her hand, afraid of drawing attention to it, and stepped to the side, forcing Rodrigo to turn them both, giving her the cover she needed.

"Uh-uh, Detective, you stay where you are. I'm leaving and will deal with you all later." He turned his head, addressing Tony as if I was the least of his problems, and right then, I might have been. "I warned Vincenzo what would happen if you refused to fall in line. You're all—" His bellow of pain cut his bitching short, and he twisted and turned, never letting go of Eden as he tried to figure out what was happening.

"Balls hot, you asshole?" she taunted as she shoved him back. He let her loose to pat his rear and between his legs, where smoke poured.

I didn't waste time; stepping to the side, I pulled out my firearm and hit him in the shoulder, causing his arm to go limp and drop his gun.

His yelling was getting distinctly higher-pitched when I kicked his legs out from under him, and he rolled on the floor, trying to put his pants out while simultaneously clutching his useless bleeding shoulder.

There wasn't enough room for the other men to get past me and to Eden, but they'd turned to face whoever had come up behind them, trusting me to take care of their girl just I had to trust that they had mine.

"You should have kept your hands off of my niece!" I shouted at the downed man. "What part of Eden fucking Moretti was off-limits, did you not understand?!" His eyes widened, full of pain and defeat, then his head jerked to the side when Eden popped off.

"Actually, it's Carlotti now. Tony and I got hitched." But that wasn't all she'd done. "Buh-bye, you rapist prick," she said sweetly with a finger wave before gripping Rodrigo's gun and putting a bullet between his eyes. Then she sat down on the steps and fished a pill out of her bra, swallowing it dry as she bitched about her feet hurting. *I really need to get those away from her...and clean this mess up before the entire police force shows up.*

"Eden!" Santos yelled, apparently done with whatever had drawn his attention away.

She looked up at him and held her arms up, confusing the shit out of me since she was supposedly married to Tony, which really irked me as I'd have zero chances of getting her away from them now, but I wasn't about to question what they had going on either. He picked her up, holding her to him, and from the grip he had, I doubted he'd be letting her go anytime soon.

"Hey, baby," she slurred, running a finger over his scars in a way that made me uncomfortable as fuck to be witnessing their reunion. "I killed your dad."

"Good, I hope it helped. God knows what he did to you. I'd have done it for you, though, angel," Santos replied, unconcerned that his father's body was on the floor next to him.

"I don't want to talk about it right now. I just want to go home," she mumbled into his neck as he carried her out of the alcove and into the main room of the club.

"Santos, where's she hurt?" Vanni asked as soon as they came into view. Marco and Tony were behind him with a restrained, pale-looking Peter between them.

"I'm not sure, but she's not talking clearly," the

scarred man answered, tucking her even closer if that were possible.

I sighed and fessed up. "She's had a few painkillers..."

"Eden, are you high or hurt?" Vanni demanded, tipping her chin up with gentle but firm fingers to look in her eyes.

She whined, "What, do you only love me when I'm sober? My feet hurt, Vanni. I needed them." Then she proceeded to pout and stare at the youngest Carlotti with liquid green eyes that had the man clearing his throat and adjusting his crotch.

"Woman, don't pull that shit right now. I need to know if you're okay."

I tried to speak up over the plainly pussy-whipped mobster, but his cousin chose to intervene.

"My Paradise better have a *damn* good reason for getting fucked up. Although I have to admit, she gave me the perfect intro." The big fucker winked at me with a crooked grin. "Hear you're family now, so I won't kill you just yet."

They're all fucking nuts, including Eden for that stunt she pulled to piss Rodrigo off. I needed a drink before my head exploded like the dead DeLuca's.

Antonio, dragging Peter along with him, joined the impromptu party, but Eden wasn't having any of that.

Eyes narrowed and looking a hell of a lot clearer

than they had moments ago, she hissed at the man. "Why are you still alive?"

"What'd he do, Eden?" the new head of the Carlottis demanded. He shook the petrified mobster before growling out, "You'd better not have touched my fucking wife, Finelli."

"You did a lot more than touch, didn't you, Peter? *'She's a feisty one, isn't she?'* Does that ring any bells? Or maybe you need to shove your dick up my ass again to jog your memory," she said, venom dripping from every word.

"Here, hold your niece, Fields," came from the enforcer as he carefully handed Eden off. I had to admit, it felt like a higher-stakes version of 'hold my beer.' I wasn't sticking around to watch what would be a grisly death; no doubt all of them would be taking a turn or three. It was time to destroy evidence and get the fuck out of the club.

"Jasper burned my foot...if you happen to come across him," Eden called over my shoulder as a bevy of armed men surrounded us to escort her out.

Eden

I watched the club burn from Marco's lap in the backseat of Tony's SUV as we pulled away. The wailing of sirens heralded the imminent arrival of the firemen that would be too late to put the blaze out. Cherry Baby and Rodrigo were truly gone, and I was free to begin a new chapter in my life with my men. One where we could be happy and thrive. Fuck anyone who didn't like it.

I wasn't seventeen and homeless. I was no longer a junkie whore. I was loved. I was cherished. And if anyone fucked with me, my men would annihilate them. Eden Moretti no longer had to struggle to exist.

My name was Eden fucking Carlotti.

epilogue

perfect

Tony

"**C**ome on, Lady Garden, water my mangrove." Marco's taunting carried a little too well, making the detective stare wide-eyed, shock and disgust warring for supremacy on his face.

"Fuck you, Marco. Do you *have* to say that? I was almost there," Vanni complained amid Eden's groan. I wasn't sure if it was annoyance or pleasure that elicited the sound, but Fields needed to go before I missed the whole thing. My dick was about to drill a hole straight through my pants, and I didn't want to miss Eden screaming around it as she came. She never failed to gush when Giovanni was in her ass.

"Why are you here, again?" I asked, turning on

the stereo to drown out the carnal soundtrack from Eden's old room.

"You said you wanted to talk to me, and I thought something was *wrong*. Don't you people have bedrooms upstairs? Jesus, why do I have to hear *that*? She's my fucking *niece*."

I had to choke back a laugh at his unintentional pun. She definitely was his niece. I had the DNA test to prove it, and there was no question about what she was currently up to.

"You could have called. I wanted to invite you on a family trip; we're giving Eden a surprise getaway— beach, drinks, and all that fun in the sun shit she's never gotten to do. If you want to go, I'll email the itinerary and tickets."

"The new boss has been riding everyone's ass, but I'm due some time off. If you're sure I'm not imposing?"

"I wouldn't have offered if I didn't mean it. You're family, even if you are a pi-cop."

My slip-up went unnoticed as *Nine Inch Nails* started their suggestive lyrics about fucking like animals just as Santos walked past the opening in the hall, butt ass naked, arms full of water bottles from the kitchen. His accessorized dick was half-hard, bobbing with every step.

"I hate you all," Fields muttered when Santos saluted him, the latter intent on getting back to Eden while the former stared at the glinting metal with a wince on his face.

"Eh, feeling's only half mutual, buddy. If you'd come work for us instead..." I hinted as I walked back toward the door, ready for his impromptu visit to end. "Call ahead next time, yeah?" I offered with a cocky grin Marco would have been proud of.

"You can count on it. I need fucking brain bleach to erase all of *that* from my head." He pointed accusingly at the hall as he stepped over the threshold.

I waved and shut the door, knowing he could see himself off the property. The guards would make sure, but it wasn't particularly needed as he wouldn't do anything to upset Eden, the last of his living family. He was continuously trying to make up for his part in past shit. Shit that I was quick to put out my mind before it could ruin our fun.

I walked into the room to find Giovanni pulling out of Eden's ass and Marco on the bottom, soaked from Eden squirting all over him. He was still in the game with a cock ring keeping him hard for Eden; he wouldn't get off until she was well sated, and that would make sure of it. The kinky fuck let her play with toys to her heart's content, and so did Vanni, for that matter. He and Marco generally paired off with Eden, and I was fine with not seeing whatever she did to them, more than I occasionally walked in on, anyway. I decided *not* to complain that I'd missed the show, just enjoying the fact that I could join in. It wasn't like I'd never get to see it again, and I could make her go off myself if I tried hard enough. As I neared, she turned drowsy green eyes my way, a smile playing around her lips just for me, lips that would be stretched around my dick soon enough. But first...

"Enjoying yourself, Eden?" I asked, already knowing damn well that she was. But I liked the confirmation, always needing to know she was good to go. We could be rough and demanding fuckers sometimes, and I never wanted her to feel pressured into anything she didn't want to do again.

"Always, boss man," she teased, knowing it irked me, but I obliged her when she tipped her head up for a kiss.

My hand threaded through her wavy black locks until my fingers burrowed down to her sweat-dampened scalp. Then my lips were on hers, gentle in juxtaposition to the grip I had on her hair.

When I released her and stepped back, lust had her pupils wider than they'd been just a moment before. She sure enjoyed a little hair pulling, a bite of pain here or there. I didn't mind providing it, none of us did, bar Santos occasionally, but he was getting to where he was more comfortable with it.

"That's husband to you, wife," I warned her as I unfastened my belt and pants, more than ready to join in.

She couldn't respond, though. Done being

ignored, Marco had thrust up into her, hard, before grinding them together to hit her piercings just right.

"You want me to take 'em out, baby? I want your ass," Santos asked, dick hard and in his hand, ready to remove the bits of metal like he usually did for anything anal. Speaking of...

"Leave them," she said with a grin as she continued to ride Marco.

I came up behind her and spread her cheeks wide to slightly pull her loosened asshole open while Santos got a condom out of the bedside drawer. We had those things *everywhere* since she got plenty of action, and it was easier than cleaning up before we were done, not that backup was bad for her birth control.

"Push it out," I demanded as I held her open. My voyeuristic tendencies had combined with occasionally directing events, and I loved to see her filled and dripping with our cum.

"Tony, you're an ass," Marco complained, knowing there was a decent chance it would hit his junk on the way down. But he'd taken that risk when he picked his position, and I didn't feel sorry for him in the least.

"Now, Eden," I ordered, letting go of one cheek to slap it before gripping it tightly again.

She complied as we all watched, except Marco. Vanni was sprawled in the chair, still flushed and not bothering to cover his junk, while both Santos and I stayed behind and a bit to the sides to have the best view.

"You're a dirty fuck, Antonio Carlotti," she harassed me as I stared at the mess sliding down her olive-toned skin.

"I'm aware, but so are you, wife," I retorted, giving her a squeeze for good measure.

Santos, running out of patience, pushed his dick into the hole I held open, edging me out of the way as he sank deep while Eden's whining, breathy moans filled the air.

"Get the fuck out of the way, Tony. Go make yourself useful elsewhere," my best friend admonished before pulling Eden up against his chest. The noises she made with the new angle had all of us pausing to check in with her. "You okay, angel?"

Refusing to open her eyes, she nodded and threaded her arms around Santos' neck, using the leverage to ride both him and Marco with an undulating roll of her hips. There wasn't much else she *could* do with the way they were plugging her lower half tight.

I watched and waited until she was close to coming before tugging her down to take my cock deep in her mouth, her screams of ecstasy muffled by the head of my dick in her throat. *Fuck I love this woman.*

Eden

As I sat under an umbrella on the private tropical beach with my back resting against Marco's chest and surrounded by my men, I decided that I had reached my version of heaven. The days following my rescue had been filled with worry over a possible pregnancy and the uncompromising restructuring of the crime lords' hierarchy. While Vinnie had made an apology for my suffering, he had adamantly refused to admit that he regretted the outcome and had even gone as far as to say it had been necessary.

The same day that I discovered that I was *not* carrying Rodrigo's child was the same day that Vinnie left the States to join his wife. I was sure that we'd all reunite at some point, but for now, the separation was for the best. Tony had been a grumpy shit for a few days, disappointed in his father's actions, but if it were my loved ones in the same position, I couldn't say that I wouldn't use anything, or anyone, to my advantage to handle the issue. Hell, I thought I'd proven that point well enough by going along with it all—other than the being sold out part. But all was well, the city was under control, and I was on my first vacation ever.

"Eden, I do not need to see your tits. Seriously, where is your damn top?" the detective, my uncle, bitched, covering his eyes as Marco's hands came up to cover said tits while I giggled at the poor man.

It was surreal to find out my mother had had an older half-brother. Apparently, it had been a shock to Fields as well, especially when he'd tracked her down only to find out she was dead, and I was...well, that I was *not* where or what he'd expected. I was *really* fucking glad I hadn't sucked his dick that night, and now I cringed a bit at how close it had been. But he'd have to get over seeing random body parts if he was going to hang around. I wasn't one for much modesty.

"It's a topless beach, man. Get over it," Vanni said from his chair behind us.

"I know, which is why my niece shouldn't be out here. All sorts of perverts could be staring at her right now—"

My giggle cut him off. "You think there are bigger pervs than these four? Besides, Santos and Tony made sure it's as private as can be, and no one is going to make it past those two." I reached over and patted the swim-trunk-clad butt of my napping husband laid out next to me on the beach blanket, earning a grunt of agreement for my trouble.

"You could have walked in on us practicing baby

making again," Santos pointed out to the highly uncomfortable detective.

"Jesus, please no. You're all a bunch of damn degenerates."

"Nah, we just know what we want. And what *I* want is to plant a baby in Lady Garden's lady garden, but she's being stubborn about it," Marco teased, surreptitiously tweaking my nipples to prove he was very much the degenerate he was accused of being.

"Excuse me, cuz? Who says you get the first baby?" Vanni demanded, sounding more than a bit put out.

"I called dibs." Marco shrugged, rubbing his sun-kissed and slightly sweaty skin against mine as my uncle decided he'd had enough of our antics and went in search of Doc, his roommate for the trip.

"But that's not fair!" Vanni whined. "Santos had her first, and Tony put a ring on it." When Marco pointedly cleared his throat, Vanni amended his statement. "Fine, Tony got to marry her, and *you* put a ring on her, which just goes to prove my point that I should get the first kid." I couldn't see him from his seat behind us, but I could imagine the pout that graced his face.

"How about a compromise since you're going to act like a little bitch about it, then? When Edie here is open for business, we can both get in there together, and may the best swimmer win," Marco offered. The man would use any excuse to double team my pussy, not that I minded in the least.

"Fine," Vanni grumbled again before threatening, "But if your big ass spawn ruins her downstairs, I'm kicking your ass."

"Hey now, no talk about that if you want me to consider popping out a kid or four. Although I'm sure Doc could glue that shit up if need be. He's fixed me up plenty before." I snickered after seeing Carlos headed our way with Fields in tow, knowing my voice would carry to him.

"There will be *no gluing* of anything, Mrs. Carlotti." I tipped my sunglasses down to glare up at him until he sighed. "I'm not an obstetrician anyhow, Miss Eden, but I don't mind being on standby in the waiting room in the event one of these boys passes out and needs attention."

Even Tony had to laugh at that one.

"Okay, Doc, but just in case you change your mind, I know where you can get some of the good shit." His groan said it all, but he was family. He wouldn't leave me hanging if I needed him. Now I just had to explain to my baby-fevered boyfriends, and husband, that it wasn't happening anytime soon.

So, that's the end. I hope you enjoyed Eden's story! As always, closing the chapter on any characters is bittersweet, but there are many new worlds to explore. Until next time!

Emma

Thank you to my, alpha, beta, and arc readers, my editor Michelle at Inked Imagination Author Services, and all of my readers who have patiently waited for Eden's conclusion to come about!

Every review counts, so if you're inclined toward reviewing, here are some handy links. Thank you!
Amazon https://books2read.com/u/b505DR
Goodreads https://www.goodreads.com/book/show/ 5775640 1-no-bad-deed
Bookbub https://www.bookbub.com/books/no-bad-deed-a-dark-mafia-romance-bad-habits-duology-book-2-by-emma-cole

Emma Cole is a multi-genre romance author covering everything from dark and light contemporary to paranormal and sci-fi. Almost all of her stories are, or will be, from the reverse harem subcategory, and none of them skimp on the heat. Emma lives in the mountains in the Northwest U.S with her kiddos and fur babies where she only puts on 'town pants' when absolutely necessary.

Follow Emma Cole

Newsletter Sign-Up. https://www.
subscribepage.com/emmacole

*Facebook Reader's Group
Emma's Author Stalkers*

Twisted Love Series
The Degradation of Shelby Ann
https://books2read.com/u/4EPlGz
The Redemption of Shelby Ann
https://books2read.com/u/me9dzz

Dark Duet
Lark
https://books2read.com/u/mv2V1V
Nightingale
https://books2read.com/Nightingale-Dark-Duet
The Complete Dark Duet Set
https://books2read.com/u/bwoWQa

Blackbriar Academy
The Order: Hit and Run
https://books2read.com/The-Order-Hit-and-Run
The Order: Ascension
https://books2read.com/The-Order-Ascension

Bad Habits Duology
No Good Deed
https://www.books2read.com/NGD
No Bad Deed
https://books2read.com/no-bad-deed

Remington Carter Series

Other Works By Emma Cole

Echoes
https://books2read.com/u/mlWGDP
Requiem
https://books2read.com/u/47EZy8

Made in the USA
Columbia, SC
23 October 2024